Sicilian Sunset

By the same author

Unbridled Love

Sicilian Sunset

Jessica Porter

ROBERT HALE · LONDON

© Jessica Porter 2009
First published in Great Britain 2009

ISBN 978-0-7090-8943-8

Robert Hale Limited
Clerkenwell House
Clerkenwell Green
London EC1R 0HT

www.halebooks.com

The right of Jessica Porter to be identified as
author of this work has been asserted by her
in accordance with the Copyright, Designs and
Patents Act 1988

2 4 6 8 10 9 7 5 3 1

Typeset in 11½/15½pt Palatino
by Derek Doyle & Associates, Shaw Heath
Printed in Great Britain by the MPG Books Group,
Bodmin and King's Lynn

CHAPTER ONE

Sarah Livingstone leaned forward and glared at her father across the boardroom table.

The other men held their breath and waited for the explosion and they weren't disappointed.

'I can't believe you want to bring a stranger in, Dad,' she yelled. Her face was purple with fury.

'Don't be ridiculous, Sarah. How can you call James Ross a stranger?'

The Head of Production stared at Sarah, 'I thought you and James were—'

Sarah cut him off in mid-sentence, 'How dare you remind me.' She pushed her chair back and stood up. 'Oh, just do what you want.' She marched out of the room.

Her father followed her. 'Wait for me, Sarah. I want some answers.' He grabbed her arm. 'What the hell is wrong with you? James is a nice bloke. If you'd married him instead of—'

'Well, I didn't, did I, and I don't want you pushing me into another relationship with him. I've told you, I've finished with men and that includes James Ross. Do what you want but leave me out of it.' Sarah pulled her arm free from his grasp and ran through the foyer doors, towards the car-park.

George Simpson stared after his daughter with a perplexed look on his face.

Sarah drove out of the gates. She pulled into a lay-by just before the main road, stopped the car and switched off the engine. She needed to get a grip on her emotions or risk having an accident. She leant her head against the side window. She was back at square one. 'The last ten years have been a complete waste of time,' she muttered, as she started up the engine again. By the time she arrived at her friend's house she was marginally calmer, but she still thought her father was wrong.

'OK. What's up?' Jane Rutherford could see Sarah was upset.

'My father. That's what.'

'What's he done now?'

'He's asked James Ross to take over as General Manager.'

'And you wanted the job?'

'No. Of course I didn't.'

'So what's the problem?'

'You know exactly what the problem is. We were an item.'

'Oh for goodness sake, that was ten years ago. Anyway, you must have known that James was the obvious choice. It's the only way your father can keep the other board members on side.'

'You've been talking to him.' Sarah stared accusingly at Jane.

'He phoned me after you disappeared. He was worried about you. For heaven's sake, grow up. The business is going through a really bad patch. The country is in the middle of the worst recession in our history. Three of the directors have threatened to resign and your father is at his wits' end. At least he's chosen someone trustworthy and someone who isn't a stranger. And he's extremely competent.'

'I suppose so,' Sarah admitted, grudgingly. 'But why on earth he's accepted the job, I do not know. How's he going to run two companies at once?'

'His mother will be looking after Sutherland Silver.'

'I suppose so,' Sarah mumbled.

'Is that all you can say? You want to be glad you haven't got my problems.'

'You? What problems can you possibly have, married to a millionaire?'

Jane's husband was an oilman from Texas. Harrison Rutherford was what they called a trouble-shooter. He was paid huge amounts of money every time he went on a job. He was an expert in his field, but the work was hard and dangerous and, according to Jane, he was away far too much.

'I might not have any money worries but money isn't everything. Pam's in trouble or at least I think she is, and if I'm right, Judith won't be able to help.'

Pam was Jane's niece. She was married to Mark Hamilton. He'd just been picked to play cricket for Lancashire. His parents were from Jamaica, but Mark had been born in Bolton. Sarah wondered if Mark had lost his job. Whatever it was, Jane was clearly worried. Pam's mother, Judith, wouldn't be any help. She'd recently got herself a toy boy and gone to live in Florida. Sarah had never known a woman as selfish as Judith. She was the exact opposite of her sister, Jane.

'So what do you think is wrong?'

'I don't actually know, but yesterday when I phoned her, she was very cagey. She sounded like she'd been crying. When I asked her if she was all right, she said she'd got a cold. Actually I'm so worried that I've decided to go over and see her.'

Pam and Mark had just bought a dilapidated farmhouse on

the outskirts of Bolton. It was only a short hop down the motorway from Jane's place in Sale.

Sarah was Pam's godmother and she knew Jane was right. There were more important things in life than worrying about James Ross. 'Can I come with you?'

'I was going to ask you if you would. I could do with some moral support because I'm hoping to persuade them to come and stay with me for the time being and you know how independent they are. I think renovating that house is turning out to be harder than they thought it was going to be.'

It wasn't long before Jane was driving down the single-track lane leading to the farm.

'You know, it is a very beautiful spot. I can understand why they bought it.'

As soon as Pam opened the door she burst into tears. Jane put her arms round her niece. 'Now then. Stop all this. Nothing can be that bad. Let's go and sit down.'

Sarah followed them into the lounge. 'What on earth is the matter?'

Pam collapsed on to the sofa. 'Oh Aunty Sarah. We've had so many things go wrong. It's awful.'

'Dry your eyes.' Jane gave her a tissue. 'Tell me what's been happening.'

'This house is cursed. Everything that could go wrong has gone wrong. I wish we'd never gone to that auction.'

Sarah could tell that Jane was thinking exactly the same thing.

'The kitchen's a mess and the bathroom's virtually unusable.'

'Well, you saw all that when you viewed it,' Jane reminded her.

'Yes, but we didn't know it had a septic tank. And we

didn't know it wasn't working properly. We can't use it.' Pam burst into tears again.

'Ah! Now that could be a problem. How are you—?'

'We've had to buy one of those portable toilets. You know. One of those horrible chemical ones they use in caravans.'

'Oh dear.'

'Oh dear! Oh dear! It's far worse than oh dear. Everyday one of us has to put the thing in the car and go and empty it.'

'Where are you taking it?' Sarah imagined she could see Mark standing on the banks of the River Irwell clutching his chemical toilet.

'There's a caravan park three miles along the main road. The owners have been fantastic. They're letting us empty it there. They've got the proper facilities. Mr Green is out with Mark at the moment, trying to find a reputable septic tank expert. He's pretty sure we won't have to have a new one. He knows a lot about them. He says the new ones aren't as good as the old Victorian brick built ones.' She started crying again. 'We didn't even know we had a septic tank.' She was so upset she was repeating herself.

'Well I'll tell you this much,' Jane's voice was firm, 'you aren't staying here a moment longer. Sarah and I will help you pack up a few things and we'll come back for the rest in a few days. We'll hire a small removal van and you can store your furniture in our barn. It's clean and dry. And don't argue. There's plenty of room at Wytcherley Hall and with Harry away so much I could really do with the company.'

When Mark arrived home it was clear from the look on his face that he was glad to see them. And he didn't even argue with Jane when she told him they were leaving.

The poor man looks exhausted, thought Sarah.

'I've told Pam we'll all come and help out with the

renovations, but until this place is fit to live in you are staying with me. It will stop me feeling lonely.'

The next few days were hectic, helping Pam and Mark to move. Sarah had no time to think about James Ross until he was due to arrive at Manchester Airport. She ended up having to go and meet him because her father was away. She thought her father had a bit of a cheek disappearing from the scene and she wondered if he'd done it on purpose.

Having parked the car, here she was, waiting for her old flame to arrive. She wondered if she'd recognize him, or even if he'd recognize her. It had been ten years since she'd seen him. However angry she felt with her father, for some inexplicable reason she'd gone to considerable trouble with her appearance. She didn't want to look old and tired. She'd done a lot of crying since Tony died. She was wearing a very elegant wool coat. She'd had her hair done and a manicure; luxuries she didn't usually have time for.

Sarah certainly didn't look old and tired. She looked about thirty when she was actually forty. Her silky blonde hair was shoulder length; her skin was like creamy porcelain and her eyes were a smoky-blue. The honey-coloured camel coat was perfect for her slim figure and quite a few men turned to have a second look as she walked past.

Then Sarah spotted James. It was easy. He was the nicest-looking man to come through the gate and by far the best dressed. He didn't look the least bit travel stained. He was wearing an immaculate charcoal suit and a perfectly pressed white shirt. His dark brown hair was short and he was slightly tanned. Sarah knew exactly why she'd had an affair with him. He was still gorgeous. She couldn't help herself. It was as though the years they'd spent apart had never happened. She ran towards him.

He dropped his bags and pulled her close, hugging her. 'It's so good to see you.' Then he held her at arm's length and stared into her eyes as though he was reading her mind. 'I'm really sorry I couldn't get to Tony's funeral. I was in Australia trying to organize our new outlets and by the time mother's letter reached me, it was too late. God knows why she didn't phone me. I would have written but I knew you would be devastated and just writing a letter seemed such an insignificant thing to do.'

'It doesn't matter,' she muttered. 'I had loads of letters and there were a lot of our friends at the service. I hardly noticed who was there and who wasn't. I was in a bit of a state.' She hurried on, eager to change the subject. 'The car is in the carpark. Would you like to go back to my place for a coffee?'

'That sounds perfect. We can catch up on all the gossip.'

Sarah was still living in the house she and Tony had bought when they got married. It was overlooking open fields and had extensive gardens.

'I thought you might have moved into a smaller house now. . . .' His voice tailed away as he realized how cruel his words would sound. Even so, he was shocked by Sarah's reaction and by the bitterness in her voice.

'You mean now that Tony's dead. Well, as a matter of fact, Tony never liked the house. He wanted a flashy apartment in the centre of Manchester. It was me who picked this and I had to really argue my case. D'you know what won him over? It was the fact that the place was a bit run down and he knew we would make a big fat profit if we did it up and sold it.' Sarah suddenly noticed James was watching her closely. She'd already said too much. If she wasn't careful he'd be asking some very embarrassing questions. 'Could we change the subject?'

'I'm sorry. Of course we can. But will you please make that drink you promised me? And could you make it a nice cup of refreshing tea instead of coffee? My mouth is so dry it feels like I've been walking in the Sahara Desert for a week.'

They were sitting in the lounge looking out across a garden that normally would have been devoid of colour. But today the winter sun splashed pale gold across a lawn sprinkled with silver frost.

James broke the uneasy silence first. 'What's all this about you not wanting me to take this job?'

Great! Dad's told him everything, thought Sarah. And now he's going to be quizzing me. 'I just didn't want someone new running things.'

'And you thought you could do the job better.'

It was a statement not a question and Sarah decided to let him think he was right. It would be much easier than telling him she didn't want to work with him because he might discover the truth about Tony's death. James had always been a bit too close to her and he was very much on her wavelength. 'Well, I'm sorry if that annoys you, but Dad insisted that you have the job and all the directors agreed. In fact, it was the only way to satisfy some of them. I've decided to go along with it so you might like to tell me what your plans are unless you're keeping them secret till the board meeting.'

'Don't be daft. I'm happy to discuss everything with you. Listen Sarah, I'm here to help you keep the firm afloat until this recession is over.'

'And what about your own company? What's happening to that?'

'Well, that's easier than you think. A few years ago we divided the company into three different corporations. We've got one outlet in America, one in Australia and Sutherland

Silver in Scotland. I've got teams of very capable people running each one. My mother is in charge of the home base. She loves making all the decisions.'

Sarah could see the advantage of having someone as shrewd as James in charge of Living Stones. She had to admit that even though it was her baby she felt relieved that she was now free to concentrate on the design side once more. Maybe life wouldn't be too bad as long as she kept James at arm's length. She had absolutely no intention of falling for his charms the second time around. As far as she was concerned, no man would ever be a part of her life again.

CHAPTER TWO

After her father asked him to act as managing director for a while, James went back home to talk to his mother about it. Then he returned in his Mercedes and he was now renting a small apartment in the centre of Manchester. It was already February and James had made a number of changes. The company was now being run on far more efficient lines and was still making a profit. It had been easy to fit into his plans and she knew her own work had improved. She'd always been an inspired designer, but the thought of Living Stones going under had preyed on her mind for the last twelve months and robbed her of any motivation. Now the inspiration was back.

James had phoned her that morning and asked her to be in his office at two o'clock. He wouldn't say why. He'd just said he had got something quite exciting to put to her. Sarah was intrigued and hurried along to his office. The door was open.

'Great. Here you are. Come in and shut the door.'

'Talking secrets are we?'

'Not quite, but until I've found out what you think I don't want anyone else listening in. Don't want them to hear me getting a roasting from the chairman's daughter.'

'Oh ha ha! Very funny! If you hadn't noticed, you're the one in charge, not me.'

'I like to think we're a team. Anyway sit down and pin back your ears.' James sounded unusually elated. 'I've had a phone call from a friend of mine, Carlo Vasari. He's putting on a big fashion show in Palma, Mallorca in a couple of months' time. It's mainly clothes, shoes and handbags, but he needs someone to provide a bit of bling appeal. He wants us to exhibit our jewellery.'

'Who did you say? Carlo who?'

'Carlo Vasari. You should know the name. He married Marilyn.'

'Oh my God. Of course. I do remember you telling me. But how can you call him a friend after he ran off with your wife?'

'Strictly speaking, he didn't run off with her, as you put it. Marilyn and I were already living apart when she met Carlo. We should never have got married in the first place. I'd just got out of the army and wanted a quiet life. She was a famous model working all over the world. We just weren't compatible. We parted on good terms but the thing that upset me at the time was that our divorce became absolute in the May and she remarried four months later. And not only that; she married a man ten years younger than herself, ditched her career, settled down and started having babies.'

'Made you feel ancient, did it?' Sarah teased him laughingly.

'Well, it didn't exactly make me feel like Leonardo DiCaprio.'

'Or even George Clooney?' giggled Sarah.

'Watch your mouth. Clooney's older than me.'

'Only by two years and you do have a look—' Sarah broke off, as James stood up and started to walk round the desk in a very threatening manner.

'OK! OK! I apologize. You're far more good-looking than George Clooney.'

James perched on the corner of the desk. 'Actually I felt quite sorry for Marilyn. There was a lot of opposition from his family. She wasn't religious; she came from a foreign country, but worst of all, she was divorced. I believe Carlo's family nearly disowned him. Then they met Marilyn and they all fell in love with her.'

'So you've got over her?'

'Maybe you helped me.'

'I always thought you were on the rebound.'

'Rubbish. I knew marriage to Marilyn was a mistake by 1995 and I didn't go out with you till 1999.'

Sarah was surprised that James was so accurate with the dates. Hurriedly she changed the subject. 'So what sort of bling does Carlo want?'

'Well, it's not so much bling he wants; he wants lavish costume jewellery. I was wondering if you could set some semi-precious stones in silver. Maybe we could combine our names and—'

'What d'you mean, combine our names?' Sarah felt apprehensive. Surely James wasn't suggesting...? No! That would be ludicrous.

James started laughing as he interpreted the look on her face correctly. 'Don't panic. I'm not thinking of marriage. What I wondered was, suppose we take our merchandise to this show as "Living Stones in Sutherland Silver" as an experiment? Although, on second thoughts, maybe marriage would be the answer to all our problems.'

'You can count your lucky stars that I know you're joking.'

'OK! OK! But what do you think about combining the names?'

'I think it sounds interesting. It will be something a bit different. High-class gems set in quality silver. Not as expensive as setting them in gold. An original idea.'

James looked delighted. He slid off the desk, grabbed her hands and pulled her up into his arms. He planted a rather passionate kiss on her lips and then he broke from the embrace. 'Whoops! Sorry! I can see the *News of the World* now. Manager takes advantage of the chairman's daughter. Oh God. Please don't sue me, Sarah.'

Sarah burst out laughing. 'You're an idiot.' But her heart was beating furiously because she'd really enjoyed the kiss. What was happening to her? 'I think I'll get back to my office and start working on some designs.'

The hours and days flew past in a haze of activity. Sarah hadn't enjoyed herself so much for years. It was just like selling her first precious piece of jewellery on that market stall in Salford, all those years ago. She'd been so proud of that bracelet. It was all her own design. Then she met Tony Livingstone and he'd persuaded her to set up in a small shop in the centre of Manchester. It was a dream that would never have come true if it hadn't been for Tony and the money he'd inherited from his father. And then it had all gone wrong and he'd been killed in a plane crash. It was so easy to start feeling sorry for herself. She pushed the miserable thoughts from her mind. After Tony's death her father had come in with her and they had expanded the business. Now she was selling her designs all over the world. And here she was on the brink of a new adventure. Her bags were packed and she was flying to Palma.

'I think I need to go to the Ladies again.' Sarah pushed her chair back and dashed away, dodging between the restaurant tables as quickly as possible.

James stared after her in consternation.

Ten minutes later she was back.

'I was just going to ask someone to go in and look for you. What's wrong?'

'I'm sorry. I'll be all right. I've just taken a couple of tablets for it.'

'For what, exactly?'

Sarah went red and leaned forward to whisper in his ear.

'You've got—'

'Shut up. I don't want everyone knowing.'

'But it must be a stomach bug you've picked up. You shouldn't be travelling.'

'It's not a stomach bug; it's nerves.'

'Nerves? How can it be nerves? You've flown hundreds of times.'

'I haven't flown since Tony. . . .' Her voice trailed away.

'Oh God. I'm so sorry. I'd forgotten. Look, don't worry: you'll be OK. You've got me to hang on to. It's just this first time that will be bad. Once you get up there you'll be fine.'

James was right. Once the plane was up in the air she started to feel better. Luckily the flight was smooth and uneventful. As they circled Palma and its surroundings, Sarah was able to enjoy the sight of the golden beaches, fringed by the deep turquoise sea and bordered with dark green pine woods.

The exhibition was being held in Pueblo Español in Palma. It was a park full of the best of Spain's architecture. The most gorgeous being a copy of Granada's Alhambra Palace with its stunning water feature.

Sarah was using some Spanish models. Five girls had on the most flamboyant flamenco dresses in flame red, deep blue, emerald green, sunflower yellow and silver white. But she hadn't chosen these models to wear her creations. Instead she had five girls dressed as men in tight-fitting black leotards. Each girl had a piece of jewellery, which matched her partner's dress.

A ruby necklace, sapphire bracelets, emeralds woven into a belt, golden topaz set in a bolero and finally a beautiful flowing bridal veil, laced with diamonds, from head to toe. None of the gems was real. That would have made the items far too expensive but they were all set in pure Sutherland Silver. All the designs were dazzling but the one that drew gasps from the audience was the veil, which was made from finespun silver, as tenuous as a spider's web.

Carlo had arranged for them to hold a viewing on the marble steps of the restaurant, with its beautiful balustrades. He'd also provided a small group of guitarists and the girls paraded down the stairs and did a small dance routine on a platform in front of the audience. It was a massive success and was attended by many international buyers. By the end of the week, the name 'Living Stones in Sutherland Silver' was on everyone's lips and the order book was full.

Before flying back to England, Carlo and Marilyn insisted on treating them to dinner, at a rather fancy restaurant in Palma. It was a chance to talk about the places they'd been to and the people they'd met.

After the meal, they said farewell and strolled down The Bourne. The soft lights spilling from the expensive shops enhanced the boulevard. The trees in the centre were filled with chattering birds, gathering to roost for the night.

James steered Sarah to a bench. 'Let's sit down and enjoy the sights for one last time. What did you think of Marilyn?'

'I thought she was lovely. It's the first time I've met her. She wasn't a bit like I expected. It's obvious she's enormously happy with Carlo and who can blame her?'

'Oh please! Not you as well!'

'What? What d'you mean?'

'Every woman who meets Carlo falls for his dark Italian looks and his blue Sicilian eyes. Even my mother is smitten.'

'I didn't know he was from Sicily and I'm not smitten by his looks,' Sarah protested, blushing. 'I just thought he had a lovely warm smile.'

'Well, I hope I'm not going to lose another woman to him.'

'What d'you mean?' Sarah frowned, not seeing where the conversation was heading.

'I mean I'm falling in love with you, Sarah, all over again.'

Before Sarah could analyse his words, James bent forward and kissed her. It was a burning kiss full of promises. Sarah felt herself responding. Her lips parted under his and her heart was beating so fast she could hardly breathe. Then suddenly she came to her senses and she pushed him away.

James grabbed her shoulders. 'What's the matter? I thought we were starting to connect. I believed you felt the same. I really believed you were falling in love with me as well.'

'No! I can't. I can't do it!' Sarah gasped. Tears were very close. 'I don't want to fall in love with you. I don't want to fall in love with anyone ever again.' And she burst into tears.

James stared at her. He was obviously bewildered. 'I don't understand. You can't let yourself be ruled by one accident of fate. Tony loved you, but he would never have wanted you to spend the rest of your life alone. For God's sake, Sarah, you're a young woman. You need to be loved. Have a family. Have a wonderful life. I can give you that wonderful life. It's what Tony would have wanted for you.'

'Tony didn't want anything of the kind for me: Tony didn't love me at all.'

James stared at her in horror. He was deeply offended by her attitude. Then he looked into her eyes and saw they had turned a deeper shade of grey. He suddenly realized there was something very wrong and he had to find out what it was. He pulled her against his chest and felt her shaking. She was in a terrible state and it was quite a while before the waves of grief subsided and she was able to talk to him.

Sarah hadn't had any intention of talking about Tony to anyone. She was ashamed by what had happened. She'd locked the memory away in the far recesses of her mind. But seeing how James was looking at her had broken the barriers down and she knew she had to tell him the truth.

'The day Tony caught that flight to New York he was leaving me, but I didn't find out until a long time after the funeral.'

James started to speak.

'Please don't say anything. Let me tell you the whole story. If you stop me I'll lose my courage and I won't be able to tell you everything. I found out he was planning to leave me when I was sorting through his clothes. There was a letter addressed to me. He'd met someone. He'd been seeing her for a year. In the letter he'd put all the details about how he wanted the house and business to be divided up. He said by the time I read it I would have had a phone call telling me where to look for it and now I would know everything. He must have intended me to get that letter more or less at the same time he landed in New York, or wherever he was heading. But obviously I never got a phone call because he never made one.'

James stared at her silently.

She rushed on with her garbled account. 'He said he'd written the letter because he couldn't deal with any upset but he wanted to make things clear to me.'

'But didn't you notice anything wrong before. . . ?' James didn't quite know how to put it.

'You mean were we OK before it all happened? It's hard to say. We'd only been married a year. He was always rather reserved and sometimes he was quite selfish. I just thought it was his upbringing. His mother never showed any affection towards him. I've often wondered what his father was like.'

'So who was she?'

'I don't know. Maybe he knew her before we got married. I tried to get some information from the airline but you know what they're like about giving out details.'

'Even if you're. . . ?'

'Yes, even though my husband had died in the crash. All I know is, that woman must have been sitting beside him. Her family might still not know she was going away with Tony. Maybe she was married too.'

'Who else knows?'

'No one.'

'What about your father?'

'Oh yes. He knows. I told him after Mum died.'

'Jane?'

'No. Just Dad and now *you* know.'

'I am so very, very sorry, Sarah. I'm very sad that you've had to keep this a secret all these years. And you know, you should have told Jane. She's your best friend.'

'I was ashamed.'

'How could you feel ashamed?'

'I thought I'd been a rubbish wife.'

'Oh Sarah! You could never have been a rubbish wife. But you are talking rubbish, that's for sure.'

'Well, now you know why I don't want to get married, ever again. And why I don't want to get involved with another man.'

'You can't tar everyone with the same brush. Not all men

are like Tony. I'm not like that and if you let me, I'll prove it to you.'

'Might take a long, long time, James.'

'I've got all the time in the world, sweetheart.'

CHAPTER THREE

They'd been back in England four weeks when James suggested a trip to Dornoch. 'We've been working really hard and I reckon we're due a break. And I'd like to see how Mother is.'

'And you definitely want me to come?'

'Yes. I think it would do us both good to get away from Manchester. Maybe a break will help us come up with some new ideas.'

Sarah wondered if she was getting in too deep with James. It was a long way to Dornoch, at least 400 miles and she'd be cooped up with him all that time.

'Oh come on, Sarah.' He grinned. 'I promise there will be no hanky-panky. You've never seen the north-east coast of Scotland. It has some glorious scenery.'

'What about all the orders we got in Mallorca?'

'Your father's got his eye on everything. There's no need to worry.'

Sarah knew he was right and it would be nice to see Elizabeth again. She pushed her few misgivings to the back of her mind and agreed to go.

'I want to stop the night at Aviemore. A friend of mine has a nice little guesthouse and I've booked us in. Oh for God's sake,

Sarah, don't look at me like that! I've booked two rooms.'

Sarah was blushing. 'Sorry! Anyway, why are we stopping at all? You used to boast you could make it from Dover to Dornoch in less than twelve hours and we've only got half as far to go.'

'Well, actually that's not strictly accurate. It's about seven hundred miles from the Channel Tunnel to Dornoch whereas it's about four hundred from here. Apart from the fact I haven't seen Alex for ages, I don't want to be crossing the Kessock Bridge at night, beautiful though it is, all lit up.'

'I didn't think you were bothered about night driving.'

'I'm not. The reason I want to get to Inverness and, for that matter, Dornoch, in daylight is because I don't want you to miss seeing some of the most fabulous scenery in the world. There are three bridges up there now. They cross over the Three Firths. One goes across the Beauly Firth. One goes across the Cromarty Firth and one goes over the Dornoch Firth. The journey between Inverness and Dornoch is now considerably shorter, thanks to these three bridges.'

'So when are we setting off?'

'Tomorrow morning about nine o'clock, if that's OK.'

'Fine. I'll just pack enough for a few days.'

'Make it enough for a week. Mother will be looking forward to entertaining us and, by the way, I'll pay the petrol and anything else. It's a way of saying thank you for supporting me in our little venture. You could have made it very difficult for me.'

'Not much point in being difficult. Not only would I have made you miserable, my dad would have been unhappy and the business could have suffered. But it's very nice of you to offer to pay for the trip and I know it would be churlish to refuse.'

*

When she got home from work, Sarah phoned Jane to let her know about the trip.

'Wow! A week alone with the tasty James Ross.'

'Oh shut up, Jane. I've already told you, I'm not interested in getting involved with another man. James and I are nothing more than friends, these days.' Sarah could hear Jane giggling. She needed to nip this in the bud now. 'And what's more, we won't be alone. His mother will be around all the time.'

'Oh dear. What a pity. By the way, does he wear a kilt at home? I could never resist a man in a kilt. So romantic, don't you think, Sarah?'

'Will you shut up? It's over between us.'

Sarah was ready, packed and waiting when James turned up the following day. As he helped her with her luggage and then held the car door open, she couldn't help thinking that Jane was right. He was very handsome. Her heart gave a little flutter. Oh my God! This is ridiculous, she thought. This is Jane's fault. She's put those ideas inside my head but she's wrong: I'm not going to fall for him again.

The journey turned out to be slightly more tedious than she expected or maybe she was tired from working too hard because she kept dozing off. They stopped for coffee several times and had lunch at Stirling. They made it to Aviemore by five o'clock and it was clear that Alex was very pleased to see James. So, after a very large evening meal, Sarah went to bed early, leaving the men reminiscing about their schooldays. From what she heard before she left the sitting-room, they'd both been at boarding school together and it sounded as bad as Colditz the way they were complaining about it.

'What school were you at with Alex?' Sarah asked later.

'Gordonstoun.'

'I didn't know you went there.'

'No I don't talk about it much.' He changed the subject skilfully. 'Look, just over there is the football stadium where Inverness Caledonian Thistle play. In a few seconds we'll be crossing the Kessock Bridge. As we cross the bridge you'll see the Beauly Firth on your left and on the right, the Moray Firth. I know I must sound like a tourist guide but I love it all so much.'

Now Sarah understood why James wanted to drive over the bridge in daylight. Luckily the sun was behind them and she could see the bridge quite clearly. Amazingly elegant, its strikingly slim towers rose high above them. Glittering steel cables linked the towers to the bridge deck.

There was a fabulous view on both sides. On her left were commercial business parks, housing complexes and a massive area of shimmering deep blue water. On the right, and as far as the eye could see, was a vast stretch of hazy blue water that sparkled like powdered sapphires. At the north end of the bridge there was a hillside on the right peppered with fabulous houses.

As they came off the bridge, James told her there was a seawater centre down on the left. 'It's just below us. Here's the entrance to it now. You can see dolphins swimming in these waters.'

'Can't we go down and have a look?' But it was too late. They had gone past it.

'Sorry. No time. Got to get to the million-dollar view before the light fades.'

'The what?'

'The million-dollar view. That's what we call it up here. I think you'll find it marked on the map simply as a scenic view. But we're now on the Black Isle and the next fabulous view is from the Cromarty Bridge.'

James was right. About ten minutes later they were sweeping down the A9 towards a really lovely low bridge running across a stretch of water that was a deep peacock blue. Sarah was entranced. She'd seen quite a lot of Britain in her time but nothing could compare to this. The skyline was dominated by row upon row of hills and mountains, stretching in an endless circle, isolating them from the rest of the world. One mountain, higher than all of them, was topped with snow. There was a patchwork of dark-green trees, apple-green meadows and fields of dazzling golden rape. And because they were quite close to the water she could see the dark powerful waves just beneath the bridge.

They followed the A9 until they had by-passed the village of Evanton. Suddenly James took a sharp left turning. 'This isn't the road I would normally take if I was in a hurry and I would never use it in the depths of winter. It takes us high up above the Cromarty Firth. Then we go even higher up and over the top of the Struie Hill and you'll be able to see the whole of the Dornoch Firth. It's the best view in the whole world. There isn't another view that can match its beauty.'

She knew what he meant by not taking the road in winter. It really was bleak and winding. Suddenly the road plunged down towards a small stone bridge. Beneath the bridge, the water tumbled at break-neck speed over the rocks.

'This is Strath Rory. You must come in summer, when it's at its best.'

Sarah's ears started to pop as the road meandered higher and higher up the hill. We must be quite high by now, she thought. Then they were over the hill and she gasped in amazement. The view was absolutely stunning. It took her breath away.

'Ah! Here we are.' The car slowed down. Nothing was coming up the hill and they veered across to the lay-by on the opposite side of the road. James parked and got out. He walked round to Sarah's door.

She hadn't moved because she was mesmerized by the panorama.

'Come on.' He helped her out and led her to the stone wall at the edge of the lay-by. 'So, what d'you think of it?'

'It's the most incredible view I've ever laid eyes on,' she whispered.

'We're lucky that the sun's shining. Sometimes it's quite misty and you can't see the mountains. The atmosphere is crystal clear today, as it often is in spring.'

Pale amethyst mountains crowded the horizon, fold upon fold stretching into the distance for miles and miles. It was like looking at a wide-screen television where the Dornoch Firth took up the whole of the picture. The Firth itself wandered in and out between the fields and small beaches. It was a truly gorgeous sea loch. Small boats out in the middle of the azure blue waters churned up trails of silver-white froth. It was every bit as beautiful as the Mediterranean.

James looked thoughtful. 'Whenever I come back from a trip abroad, if I'm driving, which I usually am, I always stop here at this spot. It's here that I know I'm home at last. I could stand here forever but we'd better get going, I think.'

They got back in the car and drove the rest of the way down to the bottom of the hill. James went left but within a few minutes he came to a small track where he was able to execute a three-point turn. 'Sorry about this. I should have turned right.'

'Don't you know your way home?' Sarah teased him.

'I just forgot there's something else I want to show you. And actually if I'd have carried on we would have eventually got to Bonar Bridge and Dornoch. It's a beautiful drive, but the road is quite narrow and very winding. This way we'll save time, but that's not why I'm doing it, I just want to take you across the last bridge.'

They were soon crossing the spectacular stretch of water that they had seen from the million-dollar view. She didn't know whether to look left or right. It was all so perfect. No wonder James had insisted on staying overnight at Aviemore. It had been a dramatic journey and by the time they pulled up outside his home she felt worn out.

His mother must have heard the car. She was outside. 'At last you've arrived. I've got the house warm and a meal waiting for you. It's lovely to see you, Sarah.' Elizabeth hugged her.

'Will you please stay for tea, Mother?' James asked her as he kissed her.

'That will be very nice. I hope you've brought some of your pieces to show me, Sarah. I know you were always a brilliant and talented designer.'

Sarah blushed with pleasure at the compliment. 'Well it seems the combination of Living Stones and Sutherland Silver is a real winner.'

'Possibly this shared venture is well overdue. I wish you two could have got together long ago.' Then she realized her *faux pas*. 'Oh dear. How senseless of me. I am so sorry about Tony. You must have been devastated. I didn't mean to be so insensitive. I'm always putting my foot in it.'

'It doesn't matter, Elizabeth. Honestly. After all, it is nearly six years since it happened.'

'I know from my own experience, it takes much longer than six years to get over the loss of a loved one.'

'Mother, I think I'd better take Sarah and her bags up to her room,' James interrupted his mother before she really put her foot in it.

'I've prepared the room overlooking the golf course, if you think that's suitable.'

'That will be perfect.' James turned to Sarah. 'You'll have a lovely view from there and it's not overlooked so you can leave your curtains open and the sun will wake you in the morning.'

'It sounds lovely,' murmured Sarah, glad to be free of the questions about Tony. She had no intention of telling Elizabeth how Tony had run off with another woman.

The room was beautiful. The wallpaper was covered with tiny sprigs of pink rosebuds. The bedlinen and curtains complimented the walls in shades of rose and lavender.

'I'm afraid this was Marilyn's idea of a perfect guestroom. I never got round to redecorating after we parted.'

'It's very pretty. It shouts Marilyn from every corner and I love it. It seems she knew what she wanted and apparently didn't let the fashion gurus sway her.'

'Perhaps you'd like to unpack. Maybe you want to shower as well. You've got a little en-suite thanks to Marilyn again. We can eat in about an hour.'

'That will be great,' sighed Sarah.

'Just wander downstairs whenever you're ready.' James left the room and closed the door. Sarah was tired but she knew a shower would revive her and it did.

The first few days were spent talking, relaxing and walking across the sandy beaches that were Dornoch's greatest asset. James took her into Dornoch Cathedral which, he proudly told her, was built in the thirteenth century. Then he spoilt it by telling her that the last witch to be tried in Scotland was put to death in Dornoch. 'She was burnt.'

They also went to Grannie's Heilan' Hame, at Embo. It was a massive campsite with a beautiful little jetty. A very adventurous family was taking a boat out into the Dornoch Firth. Nearby were some sand dunes covered with tough short grass. They stood on the edge of the grass and watched the waves lapping just below their feet.

James told her his mother was planning a small dinner party. 'I think she wants you to meet some of our friends. And it's a good excuse to entertain. The last get-together we had was Hogmanay so she's a bit bored.' He laughed.

But James wasn't laughing on the night of the party. His mother, quite oblivious to the fact that James was keen to partner Sarah, had put the object of his desire next to a family friend. Neil Anderson owned a small horse-riding establishment on the outskirts of Dornoch. He had also brought his assistant, Fiona, with him and Elizabeth had put her next to James, at the other end of the table.

Neil Anderson was tall and slim with fair hair and a deep tan obviously acquired by spending all his time out of doors. He was very attentive towards Sarah and told her he had been at school with James. He soon had her laughing at stories of how many scams the two boys had perpetrated. Several times during the meal, Sarah was puzzled to see James glaring at her from the other end of the table. Later, when the meal was over, he collared her. Neil had gone into the kitchen to top up her glass.

'What the hell d'you think you're playing at?' James whispered in her ear.

'I beg your pardon?'

'As well you might.'

'I have no idea what you're talking about.'

'You're flirting with Anderson.'

'You've got a cheek. I'm not flirting. I'm just being friendly to one of your oldest schoolfriends whom, may I remind you, your mother put next to me. And what the hell has it got to do with you if I am flirting with anyone? And why call him by his surname? What is this? Some sort of army custom?'

'He wasn't in the army with me.'

'Oh forget it. Just go away, James, or should I say Ross?' Sarah was furious. James couldn't say any more because Neil returned with the drinks. 'Oh, James, did you want a drink as well?'

'No, he doesn't,' snapped Sarah, 'and if he does he knows where the kitchen is. It's his job to look after the guests, not yours, Neil.'

Neil stared in confusion from one to the other. James stalked off. 'Oh dear. Have you two been having an argument?'

'Yes. I'm sorry I involved you. I really do apologize.' Sarah tried to pretend nothing was wrong.

'Oh don't worry. You both work together; you're bound to have the odd disagreement from time to time. James told me you were a bit uptight about him taking over, what's it called, Living Stones? You stick up to him. He's been in charge of his dad's firm too long. Everyone jumps five feet high whenever he tells them to. Be nice to see him not getting his own way all the time. He used to boss us around at school. He was what they called a natural leader. Suppose that's why he went in the army.'

'I'll remember that,' Sarah replied, only too thankful Neil hadn't heard what James had been saying.

'How long are you up here for?'

'Another few days. We're going back on Sunday.'

'Good. Then I can ask you out to dinner, can I?'

Sarah was quite surprised. They'd only just been introduced. Normally she would have declined any invitation these days, but Neil seemed very nice and she was still smarting from what James had said. 'That would be lovely. I'd love to go out.'

'Shall we say tomorrow night then? I can pick you up about eight.'

'Yes that's fine by me.'

When Sarah told James the following morning that she was going out to dinner with Neil, it went down like a lead balloon.

'I knew you were flirting with him,' James growled.

'I told you last night, it's nothing to do with you. What on earth have you got against him anyway?'

'I've got nothing against him, but I had hoped you and I—'

Sarah cut him off. 'I don't think it's a good idea to reignite old passions. They never turn out right. We had one fling and it didn't work.' She tried to be a bit gentler with him. 'Listen, I know you want to look after me, but I find it embarrassing that you know how Tony treated me. And I don't actually want another serious affair. I'm going out with Neil on a purely platonic basis and at least he doesn't know what a failure I was as a wife.'

James could see that Tony had really wounded her, but he had one last piece of advice. 'Well I hope you make it clear to Neil that you don't want a serious relationship because you're a very beautiful woman, Sarah and I think he's smitten.'

Sarah was feeling a bit fed-up with everyone trying to sort out her life. First her dad, then Jane and now James. This was exactly why she jumped at the chance of going out with a stranger. And she wanted to feel worthwhile. Tony had taken away her confidence where men were concerned.

She dressed with care. She wanted to look her best and when she saw the look on Neil's face she knew she had succeeded. The restaurant and the meal were lovely, but finally she was back in Neil's small sports car. When they arrived at the house, he turned off the engine, leaned over and started to kiss her and they weren't just friendly kisses. Sarah could tell he was quite wound up. It was obvious that Neil thought she was looking for a bit more than just fun. His kisses were stirring her senses and she was starting to enjoy them.

'Let's go to my place,' he whispered in her ear.

She suddenly realized she'd made a big mistake going out with him. 'No!' Sarah gasped. She pulled away from him, grabbed the door handle and fell out of the car. She was on her feet and running up the path before Neil had time to react. As Sarah reached the door, it opened and she collapsed into the hall.

James must have heard the car draw up because he was just behind the door. 'What the hell has he done to you?' He was furious.

'Nothing! Wait!' She tried to grab his arm, but James was off down the path.

Neil was just coming through the gate when James hit him.

'No! No!' Sarah screamed. 'He hasn't done anything.'

Suddenly she was thrust aside as Elizabeth pushed past her, strode down the path, grabbed both men and shouted at them.

Neil hurried to his car, got in and drove away.

James marched into the house and, without a word, disappeared up the stairs.

Elizabeth turned to Sarah. 'What a good job I came over with this cake.' The tone of her voice was icy. 'I never thought I would see my son brawling over a woman and I don't like it. I hope you can sort this out, Sarah.' She went off down the path.

Sarah burst into tears as she closed the door.

The next morning both James and Sarah looked as though neither of them had slept and they hadn't. Sarah placed the coffee jug on the table and sat down. 'We have to talk.'

'Damn right about that,' snarled James.

'You can't blame Neil. It was my fault. I might have led him on. I'm just not used to the dating game anymore. I never thought I'd have to go through all that messy stuff again.' Suddenly there were tears in her eyes. 'You were right about it all.'

James melted. 'No, I wasn't right. I was totally out of order about everything. I'm sorry, Sarah and now I'm also going to have to go and apologize to my best friend.'

'He didn't really do anything. He only kissed me, but we both got a bit carried away and then I couldn't. . . .' Her voice tailed away. 'It must have been so humiliating for him. We both have to apologize. I'll come with you.'

Neil was at his stables. 'Wait in the car,' said James. 'I'll go first then if he has a pop at me you can come and rescue me.'

Sarah watched the two men anxiously and wondered what they were saying. She hoped Neil didn't want his revenge. He was perfectly entitled to 'take a pop' as James had put it. She really wished she'd never accepted his invitation.

'What the hell did you think you were doing?' Neil had a bruise below his eye.

'I'm truly sorry, mate. Honestly! I just lost it. I thought you had. . . .' James couldn't say it because he knew that his friend wasn't that sort of man.

'I thought all the signals were at green. You know she doesn't exactly act like a nun. We'd been having a great time all night. Then she suddenly turned all scared, like. I mean, let's face it, she has been married. She knows what it's all about.'

'It was a bad marriage.' The words slipped out before James could stop himself. 'Listen, Neil. Don't tell her or anyone what I've just said.'

'But she told me her husband was killed in a plane crash.'

'Yes, but I bet she didn't tell you he was going off with another woman on that plane, did she?'

'Oh hell. I'm so sorry. I knew she was a nice woman. I thought all that flirting didn't ring true. And then leading me on just to dump me. No! I knew it didn't feel right. I don't mind telling you, James, after all this time on my own, she's a woman I could fall in love with.'

'Well you can join the end of the queue.'

'You're in love with her too? Well! May the best man win.'

'That will be me then, since I'll get to see more of her than you will. Anyway she's waiting in the car. Wants to apologize as well. Remember! Don't mention anything about Tony. She would be so humiliated to know I'd told you.'

'Don't worry. I won't ever say a word. That Tony must have been a real jerk.'

'I think he was the biggest jerk in the world,' agreed James. 'From what Sarah has told me, he wasn't a nice bloke. I don't think he was right for her.'

Sarah walked slowly towards Neil wondering how she could put things right.

He just shook his head at her and smiled. 'We've all been prize idiots.' Neil pulled her into his arms and gave her a quick hug. 'I made a real fool of myself. I don't usually do that on a first date. It must have been your perfume.'

Sarah couldn't help smiling. 'That's a first. I'm so sorry. I've been really confused since Tony died. Being a widow takes a bit of getting used to and I am obviously not ready to get back in the market-place,' she joked.

'You just let me know as soon as you are and I'll come running. Just give me a chance against that handsome bloke over there. You're a beautiful woman, Sarah. Don't shut yourself away. Don't waste your life in the past. Be a long time before you die.'

'I hope so! Thank you for understanding. I won't forget what you've said.'

She walked back to the car and got in. She was pretty quiet on the way back.

'What's up?'

'Got one more person to apologize to and I'm dreading it.'

'Mother!' James sighed. 'You and me both. Better get it over with then.'

Elizabeth accepted their apologies with a good grace but the incident had spoiled things between the two women. Sarah was glad when it was time to pack up and go back to Manchester.

CHAPTER FOUR

Keeping James at arm's length was very difficult especially as they were spending a lot of time together. He had come up with another sensational idea. He wanted to exhibit the new collection at a big gem fair in Milan. Sarah wasn't sure about it because she knew it would mean that she and James would be together day and night for two weeks. But in the end she gave in. She knew that Elizabeth Ross would be joining them and James wanted to take a few more of their staff along. 'Got to have plenty of workers to take all the orders,' he joked. So maybe he would stick to the business in hand.

Their designs were just as popular as they had been in Mallorca and they found themselves frantically trying to fit in a great many private viewings. Sarah could hardly believe that from worrying about Living Stones going under, her designs were getting rave reviews. They worked well together and it seemed like he'd put the idea of a romance with her out of his mind.

Everything went quite smoothly until one of Tony's friends turned up at the exhibition. Louis Philippe was one of the richest men in France. He drifted around exhibition after exhibition, constantly on the lookout for good quality gems in which to invest. Strictly speaking he was a fashion designer but he came from a rich family. It was well known, in the circles in which he moved, that he really didn't need to work at all.

'My dear Sarah.' Louis kissed her hand. 'I miss Tony so much.'

Louis had taken the trouble to fly from America to England for Tony's funeral so Sarah knew he was sincere about missing him. He had also tried to buy Living Stones from Sarah. Her father had persuaded her not to sell. After Louis had gone he had told Sarah that hell would freeze over before he'd let the company go to Louis. Sarah tried to find out why her father was so much against the Frenchman but he refused to talk about it. She knew her father had never liked Tony and now it seemed he didn't like any of his friends either. Maybe her father was clairvoyant. He'd been right not to like her husband.

'I was very surprised to hear you had hitched your star to Sutherland Silver.'

'I haven't "hitched my star" as you put it, to anything. James and I have just joined forces for a few exhibitions. We are both trying to avoid going bust during these troubled times. There's nothing legally binding about the set-up. They're still separate companies.'

'Ah! Yes! These are dark days indeed but you know you could have come to me. I would do anything for you. Tony would have wanted me to watch over you. I made that offer for Living Stones at the funeral in good faith. I put my reputation on the line. Some people might have thought I was taking advantage of you at such a sad time; but I only had your happiness in mind. I was a bit upset that you declined my generous offer.'

Sarah could see James pulling faces behind Louis's back.

'May I treat you to dinner tonight, my dear, to make up for everything?'

'No! Don't go!' James was mouthing.

Sarah was furious that James was trying to organize her life yet again. Maybe this was a chance to show him, once and for all, that she wasn't interested in a romance with him. Quickly and without any further thought, she accepted Louis' invitation. It gave her quite a bit of satisfaction to see the look of horror on James's face.

'Excellent. I'll have my driver pick you up at eight o'clock.' Louis waltzed out of their exhibition suite, meeting Elizabeth in the doorway. 'Elizabeth, looking divine as usual.' Louis kissed her hand.

'How wonderful to see you again, Louis.' Elizabeth also knew the Frenchman and was quite eager to talk to him so she didn't notice the row going on between her son and Sarah, at the other end of the room.

James was arguing in undertones with Sarah. 'You can't possibly go to dinner with him.'

'I beg your pardon, James?' Sarah's voice was icy.

James was too preoccupied to notice. 'He's got a terrible reputation.'

'Reputation? What the hell are you talking about? I've known Louis for ages. He and Tony were really good friends.'

'Everyone reckons he's mixed up in the underworld.'

Sarah burst out laughing. 'Don't talk rubbish. What film do you think you're in? *The French Connection*?'

'It's not a joke. You mustn't go out with him.'

'Don't try and run my life,' Sarah's voice rose.

Elizabeth, who had just kissed Louis goodbye, hurried over. 'What's going on?'

'Nothing,' muttered Sarah, flushed with anger.

'Sarah is going out to dinner with Louis, Mother.'

Elizabeth raised her eyebrows. 'I should think Sarah can go out with whom she pleases. And now, can we close up and go back to our hotel, please?'

There was an uncomfortable silence in the taxi. Sarah ignored James. James stared out of the window. And Elizabeth just leaned back and closed her eyes.

It was almost eight o'clock and Sarah was still seething. She intended to show James that he couldn't dictate to her what she could or couldn't do. She was just about ready when there was a knock on the door. Good! It would be her lift. But it wasn't: it was James.

He looked at the low-cut black dress and scowled. 'I see you're going then.'

'Apparently.'

'Well, don't blame me if he makes a move on you.'

'Don't be bloody ridiculous. He wouldn't do that, especially knowing Tony.'

'In case you haven't noticed, Tony's no longer around to protect you.'

Sarah's eyes turned steel grey. 'It's good of you to remind me. But let me tell you something: I don't need protecting. I'm a grown woman; I can protect myself. Shut the door when you leave.' She grabbed her coat and bag. Then she stalked off down the corridor, intending to wait for her lift in the foyer, well away from James.

She saw Louis's driver arrive in the foyer and waved to him. He escorted her out to the flashy Mercedes, which was one of the many cars that Louis owned. She settled herself in the back seat and wondered which plush restaurant Louis was using tonight. He was known for eating out at the most expensive places in every European city.

She was surprised when the chauffeur pulled up at the

front of the hotel where she knew Louis was staying. Maybe they were picking him up. But no. The chauffeur was holding the door open for her. Not wanting to make a fuss in public, Sarah followed him into the foyer and then into the elevator, which stopped at the fifth floor.

'Ah! Sarah! Welcome! I thought it would be nice to eat in private. Therefore I have asked the hotel manager to provide something simple but delectable. I have also handpicked the people who will serve us our food. I have used this hotel for years and it is the best in Europe.'

Sarah was quite taken aback to find she was dining alone with him. She almost turned tail, but then good sense prevailed. She wasn't actually alone. Half the hotel's staff seemed to be hovering, one man already having taken her coat.

'Please come and sit beside me.' He led her to a pale-green velvet settee. 'Perhaps a small glass of champagne before the meal.'

The waiter glided over with the bottle. He poured some into each glass. 'How do you like this room?'

Sarah glanced round. There was a bit too much gold leaf for her taste but she didn't say so. 'It's beautiful.'

'I'm glad you like it. Now, I have chosen our food myself. I think you might like the fresh salmon in a white wine sauce perhaps followed by the raspberry tartlets topped with fresh whipped cream. But if there is anything that you don't like please say so and the manager will bring a menu. I only asked for two courses. I didn't want you to feel, how do they say, bloated. I always think it can spoil the rest of the evening.'

Sarah wondered what he meant by 'the rest of the evening' as alarm bells started to ring. Don't be ridiculous, she told herself. Louis has always been a perfect gentleman.

The meal was excellent and Louis kept her entertained with

stories about his childhood in Paris. 'You should come and see my house and the place where I design fabulous gowns for the richest ladies in the world.'

Sarah knew it wasn't just a house he owned in France. It was a great big gorgeous château, built by his ancestors in the seventeenth century.

Louis got up from the table and came and stood behind her. Then, to her great consternation, he bent down and kissed one of her bare shoulders. 'Go and freshen up, my dear, while I change into something more appropriate.' He disappeared into the bedroom.

For one moment, Sarah felt absolutely paralysed as she noticed the staff had left and they were totally alone. Then her brain clicked back into gear. For the second time that night she grabbed her coat and bag and quietly left the suite of rooms. She could either wait for the lift or take the stairs. She felt sick with fear as she anticipated the long wait for the lift to arrive. She bolted through the door leading to the stairs. As soon as the door swung to behind her, she bent down and took off her shoes. Then she sped silently down to the ground floor. Slipping her shoes back on, she opened the door, spotted the exit opposite and dashed across the foyer out into the fresh air.

But once she was outside she realized what a pickle she was in. First of all, she didn't have any money with her. Her tiny evening purse contained just a lipstick, powder compact, handkerchief and her phone. She was in a strange city: she was alone, with no money for a taxi. This was a dangerous situation and Sarah knew there was only one thing to do. She went back inside the hotel and looked around for somewhere to hide from Louis. She spotted what looked like a window seat lurking behind some curtains and dodged behind them and sat down. Then she got out her phone and dialled the number. 'Please answer the phone, James,' she whispered, crossing her fingers and peering through the thick velour curtains. She heard the ring tone. No sign of Louis.

'Hello, Sarah. What's up?'

'Help me, James,' she whispered into the phone.

'What? Can you speak up? I can hardly hear you.'

She took a chance and raised her voice. As quickly as possible she gave him the name of the hotel and told him what had happened. 'I'm hiding in the foyer. Behind some red velvet curtains near the desk. Please come and get me. Hurry. Please.'

Suddenly James grasped what had happened to her. 'Stay exactly where you are. I'm on my way. It isn't far. Just sit tight.'

The next ten minutes seemed like ten years to Sarah. Then the curtain was pulled back. She just stopped herself from screaming because the face looking down at her belonged not to Louis but to James, thank God.

'Come on. Quick. Let's get out.' He grabbed her arm and dragged her out into the waiting taxi. 'Got a taxi here. It was quicker than getting my car out of the car-park.'

Sarah collapsed into his arms as he told the driver to take them back to their hotel. She couldn't help herself and burst into tears. 'Please don't say I told you so.'

'I'm not going to say anything till I get you back into your room and neither are you.' He inclined his head at the driver.

Obviously he doesn't want a scene in the car, thought Sarah.

By the time they reached her room she'd calmed down and she was able to give him all the gory details.

James was furious. 'I'm going to fix that bastard once and for all.'

'No! No! Please don't make a fuss. He'll only deny it.

There's no proof he was going to do anything wrong. He can say it was all in my imagination.'

'It's against my better judgement, but I'll leave him alone as long as he stays away from you.'

'And please don't tell your mother about this. She's already disgusted about what happened with Neil. I couldn't bear it if she knew about Louis.'

CHAPTER FIVE

As it happened, there was no sign of Louis at the exhibition the next day or for the rest of the second week. Two days before the exhibition ended the organizers threw a party for all the exhibitors and their staff. James tried to get Sarah to go with him, but she had no intention of letting him feel sorry for her. She declined. 'I'm sorry but I'm going out to dinner that night.'

James groaned. 'Who with this time?'

'Maurice Cresson. So, this time, as you put it, you don't need to worry.' Elizabeth looked up from the croissant she was about to break open. 'What's that, dearie? Are you going out with Maurice now?'

'Mother. I don't think we should be quizzing Sarah like this.'

'I thought she was going out with Louis.'

Sarah gasped. So James had told his mother after all. 'Please excuse me. I want to go and get a newspaper.'

'But you haven't finished your breakfast,' Elizabeth said sweetly, as if she knew exactly what was going through Sarah's mind.

'I'm suddenly not hungry,' Sarah snapped disappearing out of the dining-room.

'Wait for me.' James came running after her. 'Listen, Sarah, I swear I didn't tell her. Honestly.'

'Well someone did.'

'Look. She was there when he asked you out. That's all she knows. I swear.'

But Sarah didn't believe him. And she wasn't actually going out with Maurice, which was a pity since he was a very nice man. He was the top diamond cutter for De Beers. He was also French like Louis but his manners were impeccable. He was fifty-five and a widower. His wife had died in a car crash and Sarah had a special fondness for him. In fact, he'd asked her to the party already, but she just didn't feel she could go through another evening of Elizabeth's pointed looks again. So she'd told Maurice that she was going to dinner with James on the night of the party.

If she hadn't been in such a state, Sarah would have realized that she was bound to be caught out, especially when the two men were both going to that same party.

'Good evening, James. Nice kilt.'

James smiled at him. 'Well this is something a Frenchman can't get away with so that ought to even the score between us. Where's Sarah, by the way?'

Maurice looked puzzled. 'Not with me. What are you talking about? She's with you. Is she not?'

James stopped dead in his tracks. 'She told me she was having dinner with you.'

'So she has a secret assignation she doesn't want either of us to know about. She told me she was having dinner with you. Maybe she's out with Louis.'

'No! Not at all. There's no way!' He saw Maurice's surprised look and he knew he had to tell him.

'Well! The little rat. I've never liked the man. He's got connections to—'

James cut him off. 'Yes. I know. Let's not mention it here. You don't know who's listening. I tried to tell Sarah but she didn't believe me. He was one of Tony's friends and that's not saying much.'

Maurice raised his eyebrows.

Here we go again, thought James. Too many people are getting to know Sarah's private business. But there was no way out of this now so he told Maurice about Tony's betrayal and swore him to secrecy. 'She's had a really bad time recently. I know she's not out with Louis, but I bet I know where she is.'

'Where?'

'I'll bet anything she's sitting in her hotel room licking her wounds.'

'So you'll go and fetch her, will you, James?'

'I'll have a damn good try.'

'Good luck. She's a very nice lady. She doesn't deserve all this unhappiness.'

James was right. He found Sarah in her hotel room. 'How on earth did you think you were going to get away with the lies, Sarah? We were both at the party.'

She grinned sheepishly. She was wearing a silk kimono and she pulled the belt tighter. 'Never thought about that. I didn't want to go to the party and obviously I was clutching at straws. Any port in a storm, as they say.'

'Why didn't you want to go to the party?'

'Because I couldn't stand to see how your mother thinks I'm some sort of floozy and I was scared I might see Louis.'

'My mother doesn't think that about you and I happen to know that Louis went back to Paris the day after you ran out on him.' He moved closer to her and pulled her into his arms. 'You've got to stop beating yourself up over Tony. We aren't all like him or Louis for that matter. Some of us are decent, kind men, like me, or devilishly good-looking boys like Neil, who just happen to be in love with you.'

So now Sarah knew for sure that James was in love with her, as she had already begun to suspect. Looking up into his dark-brown eyes she felt her heartbeat quicken. There was a question in those eyes. They were asking her if she loved him? Maybe it was time to test the water. She couldn't help smiling at him.

It was the answer he wanted and he bent his head to claim her lips.

Sarah opened her mouth to the sweetness of his tongue and leaned against him to enjoy their first real kiss for over ten years. He hadn't lost his expertise and she gasped as his hands caressed her body through the paper-thin gown. Floating on air, she was utterly breathless with longing as his hands lingered on her breasts before slipping down to her waist. His lips were now exploring her neck and she leaned back so she could enjoy the exquisite sensation. She ran her fingers through his hair. Because she was desperate for his hands to continue the journey downwards, she moved even closer to him. It was a sensual invitation executed deliberately to let James know she was ready for the next step. His whole body stiffened and Sarah knew that her action had inflamed him, but it wasn't meant just to tease: she really wanted him to accept what she was offering him. But he didn't.

Gently he pushed her away. 'I don't want us to rush things, Sarah. I think we both need some more time because I don't intend this to be a casual affair. I want it to be forever. So go and get your glad rags on because I'm now going to drag you to that party. While you get changed I'll try and recover my composure. I know exactly what you were up to and I think you probably know it certainly worked, but next time you do it, I won't let you get away with it.'

'Then I should tell you, I'm already looking forward to the next time.'

Sarah enjoyed the party in the end and two days later they packed up, ready to set off, back to the Channel Tunnel. Sarah and James were travelling together in his Mercedes. His mother was going back with some of the staff from the Dornoch base. She had travelled to Milan with them because she didn't like flying on her own.

Well, at least she doesn't have to be in the same car as a floozy, Sarah thought to herself, but she didn't say as much to James. The others had left at first light, but James insisted on having a proper breakfast. 'We've got several days' driving ahead of us and we're not going to rush at it like a bull at a gate. I intend taking my time. These exhibitions are hard work. I'm feeling worn-out.'

Once breakfast was over, they returned to their rooms, finished packing and then James called the porter to let him know their bags were ready to go out to the car, which was down in the underground carport. They were at the desk paying for their stay when Sarah noticed a slight altercation between one of the porters and the hotel manager. Then the manager walked over.

'Sir. I think we have a bit of a problem.'

James looked puzzled. 'My credit card's gone through all right. Your receptionist has just given it back.' He started fishing in his wallet.

The manager put a hand on his arm. 'The problem is not with the card. The problem is with your car, sir. The porters have just taken your bags out.'

'Oh no!' Sarah gasped. 'The car hasn't been stolen, surely?'

'Will you please come with me? Sir, madam.'

They followed the manager into the elevator. When they reached the carport, the manager led them to where the staff had presumably parked their car two weeks ago. Two porters were standing guard over the bags.

Sarah felt an inexplicable desire to laugh, which was possibly the onset of hysteria. Then she suddenly realized how scary this was. Instead of the ten-year-old sand-coloured Mercedes that James was so fond of, there was a large neat square box of metal which looked suspiciously like a car that had been crushed. She knew instantly who was responsible. The tears welled up. It was all her fault. This was payback time. This was all down to Louis Philippe. She suddenly felt sick with terror.

'We've called the police. We've got no idea how this has happened. This carport is one of the most secure in the city. I can only apologize on behalf of the management.' The manager looked like he was going to cry.

'It's not your fault,' James assured him.

'We can go back to my office and wait for the police. I will provide you with rooms, free of charge, while this is sorted out. Please come with me.'

As soon as they had a moment alone, James told Sarah what was going to happen next. 'We aren't going straight back to England. We're going to Rome. No! Don't interrupt me. I've got to tell you before the manager returns. We know who is behind this and the police won't be able to do a thing so we don't tell them anything. Let them assume it's been done by mistake: a gang that's got the wrong car. Then we go to Rome to see Carlo. He has the means to sort this out. We don't need to phone Mother or anyone else. We'll be flying home and might possibly be there at the same time they arrive.'

Sarah wanted to ask him what 'means' Carlo had, but the manager returned.

It took all morning to sort things out with the police and the insurance company. They declined the offer of rooms for the night and were at last on their way to the airport in a taxi, which the manager insisted would be paid for by the hotel. James wouldn't talk in the taxi. 'Leave it, Sarah. I just need to put my thoughts in order.'

By the time they were seated in one of the airport cafés she was in tears. 'I know you don't want to talk to me, but I've got to tell you how sorry I am.'

'Oh good God, Sarah. I'm not blaming you.'

'But you didn't want to speak to me in the taxi.'

'Only because I didn't want the driver to hear me. That's all.'

'But he didn't know us.'

'We don't know that. Actually that wasn't an ordinary taxi; it was one of the chauffeur-driven cars laid on by the hotel for special guests. The driver would be one of their employees.'

Sarah gasped. 'But surely you don't think the hotel was involved?'

'Not the management, but someone must have known how to override the carport security and they must have had help from one of the staff. Anyone could have been paid and if they were offered a lot of money, well—'

'Everyone has their price,' Sarah finished the sentence for him.

'Correct! Now, I'm going to leave you here to guard our bags whilst I traipse round the various airline desks and try and find the earliest flight I can.'

'James, do you know where Carlo lives?'

'Of course I do. I've never been but I've got his address.'

James was back within twenty minutes. 'I've booked us on a flight at four o'clock. We land in Rome at approximately half past five. We can get a taxi to the Palazzo Vasari. And we should be there by seven, although I'm only guessing. It depends how easy it is to get a taxi and it depends exactly where Carlo's place is. We're landing at Fiumicino Airport, which is twenty miles from the centre but Carlo might live on the opposite side of the city.'

For the first time that day everything went according to plan and by 7.30 they were standing outside the gates of the magnificent Vasari residence. The taxi drove off at speed. James and Sarah stared after it in amazement.

'Blimey,' said James. 'I know Italians like to drive fast, but that's ridiculous. He barely looked at the money I handed him. He couldn't get away quick enough.'

'Maybe he wants to get back to the airport for another fare.'

'Mmm!' James murmured, then he turned and rang the bell.

A young fellow came out of a small building at the side of the locked gates. 'We would like to see Mr and Mrs Vasari,' said James in Italian.

'No callers,' the Italian said, and turned away.

'Wait,' shouted James. 'Tell him James Ross is at the gates. He knows me.'

The man turned back, looked them up and down and then he marched off towards the house.

Sarah wished she could speak Italian as fluently as James. She'd listened to him chattering away with the waiters at their hotel and had felt really envious. 'What did you say?'

'Just asked if I could see Carlo. Told him to tell Carlo my name.'

'I've often wondered how you can speak so many languages so fluently. I've heard you speak Spanish and I've heard you speaking French to Louis Philippe.'

'Just a hobby of mine at school.'

Their conversation was interrupted by shrieks of delight as they saw Carlo and Marilyn running down the drive followed by several servants.

'They might not be so pleased to see us when they know why we've come,' muttered James.

To Sarah's utter distress, as soon as the gates were unlocked, she burst into tears.

Marilyn threw her arms around her. 'Oh my dear Sarah. What on earth has happened?'

'Never mind about that now,' said James. 'Let's get her into the house. You can ask us as many questions as you want when Sarah's calmed down.'

While Marilyn comforted Sarah on the settee, James and Carlo disappeared into another room. 'Darling, Sarah, tell me what's happened. Why are you here?'

'I feel such a fool, Marilyn. It's all my fault. We're in great danger and it's all my fault.' The whole story came flooding out, swimming on another deluge of tears.

Marilyn was horrified. 'That's awful. That horrible man. I never cared for him. He comes smarming round Carlo whenever we're at any receptions. Carlo doesn't like him either. But I never dreamed he would try and lure a woman into his rooms.'

'Maybe if I'd just acted normally and said I wanted to go, it might have been OK. I mean I didn't give him much chance to explain himself: I just bolted.'

'Well, he must have been keen to do something because, like you say, all the waiters had disappeared. And to do something like that to the car. He must have terrific powers. I mean, that hotel car-park is like Fort Knox. Carlo always insists we stay there if we go to Milan.'

The two men were suddenly back in the room.

'Dry your eyes, Sarah.' Carlo came over and sat down at the other side of her. He got hold of her hands. 'I am going to sort out that nasty little Frenchman.'

'But James says he's dangerous.'

'I know exactly how dangerous he is, but, more to the point, he knows I am potentially even more dangerous. Now, I've organized some rooms for you both. You are going to stay for a few days while I sort everything out. We will enjoy having you.'

Their time at the Vasari Palace passed in a whirl. Marilyn showed them round. The house was full of beautiful paintings, sculptures and furniture. Most of the reception rooms on the first floor were painted in vibrant colours. The room they were in, for instance, had a whole wall devoted to what looked like the Virgin Mary ascending into heaven. Her long flowing robes were a vivid rich red. It was the colour much favoured by Titian; so much so, it had been named after him. There were cherubs floating on fluffy clouds in a golden sky. Sarah wondered if Titian had actually painted it because she had seen something remarkably like it in a church in Venice and that had been painted by him.

Marilyn didn't tell her who had painted it. Maybe she didn't want to boast, or maybe she didn't know. It was just like a film set, but Sarah knew what she was seeing was the real McCoy and Palazzo Vasari was the home of a millionaire. But even that knowledge didn't prepare her for their flight home.

CHAPTER SIX

Sarah couldn't believe she was sitting in a private jet, owned by Carlo, flying from Rome's Ciampino Airport and the only other passenger was James. She looked across at him. He didn't look fazed at all; he looked as though this sort of thing happened to him every day of the week.

'What's the matter, Sarah? Don't you like our new mode of transport?'

'I can't believe you're so calm,' she spluttered.

'Ater all that's happened to both of us over the last ten days, I'm just glad to be up in the air and safe from those French thugs.'

'But . . . but. . . .'

'Come on, spit it out.'

'How can Carlo afford something like this?'

'He's a very rich man. In fact, the whole of his family is rich beyond our understanding. On a par with the oil barons of Kuwait, I imagine. However, you can lease aircraft like this, you know.'

'So has he leased it just to fly us home?'

'No,' James was forced to admit, with a smile. 'It does belong to him, or rather to the business.'

'My God! And how much has it cost him?'

'Do you think I would be rude enough to ask him that?'

'Oh, come on! Boys and their toys! Of course you've asked him.'

'Oh all right. Yes, I did. This is a Boeing Business Jet and a new one would cost anything from forty to fifty million dollars but—'

'Oh my God!'

'Will you let me finish? This isn't new. It's ten years old. Carlo's family and business associates, shared the cost, and bought it for twenty million dollars.'

'Oh wow! What a bargain! Got it on eBay, did they?'

'Don't get smart. Anyway, look, the cabin steward is coming, so drop the subject. It's not nice to talk about Carlo's personal business especially when he's doing us so many favours.'

Sarah was forced to do as he asked but she still found it difficult to accept that a family that was only in the fashion business, could afford something like this. It might be a second-hand bargain, but the fuel alone must be costing another small fortune. She wondered if. . . . No! Forget it, she thought to herself, before her curiosity took her to a rather nasty place. She wiped the thoughts from her mind and instead she asked James what they were going to tell his mother, and everyone else, for that matter, when they showed up in a taxi and without the Mercedes.

It was June and the two companies were flourishing. It seemed they must have set their prices at just the right level because, in spite of the recession, sales were up. They had continued with the theme 'Living Stones in Sutherland Silver' and it was this particular line that was attracting most interest. There had been one or two favourable reports in certain fashion magazines.

Then Sarah had been asked to do an interview about why the two companies were doing so well when quite a number of diamond outlets had gone to the wall. Sarah explained that she thought costume jewellery was taking over from the real thing. There had been a spate of thefts at various holiday hotspots all round the world. She said that people weren't as worried if they only had relatively cheap pieces stolen and they weren't paying extortionate insurance policies for them. And it meant that most people could just put their diamonds in a safe or the bank and forget about them.

The only fly in the ointment was that Sarah had to send her gems together with the new designs up to Dornoch every month. They were employing a driver because neither George nor James trusted independent carriers; they never seemed to get there on time.

Sarah felt the same way, but she was sorry that they'd only been able to employ one driver because today he was in hospital with a broken leg. She was trying to work out who to send up to Scotland in his place and it wasn't easy. She didn't think it was right to send anyone who had a family. They worked hard enough as it was without being asked to go away for a few days. Some of them had already been to the shows in Spain and Italy this year and she knew it wasn't fair to ask them to stand in for Peter. In any case, he was going to be off sick for quite a while so this was going to be a long-term problem. And until they could get hold of another driver, she knew in her heart that there was only one person she could ask today: herself!

So here she was: driving the proverbial white van 400 miles up the country. The weather was superb and so was the scenery. She'd set off at eight o'clock, had one coffee break and now she was snatching a sandwich at Stirling. By four o'clock she was at Inverness having her last break and keeping her eye on the van from the window of the café. Even though it was locked, she had hardly let it out of her sight all day. The contents weren't worth an enormous amount of money. There were the boxes of loose semi-precious stones and they were insured for the cost of buying them in again. And then there were her folders containing the latest designs, which were actually worthless to anyone else. Obviously the insurance company wouldn't be very pleased if they had to replace the van. But it would be even worse if she had to redo her designs. It would take her a long time and she could do without the inconvenience.

By the time she arrived at Dornoch she was tired and she felt grubby but she was very pleased to see James.

'Got your room ready. Go and have a shower. I'm making a light tea. You look like you'll need an early night. It was really good of you to do this. We are quite desperate for all this stuff. How's Peter doing?'

'He's at home now and he's bored out of his mind. His wife's keeping tabs on him. It'll be a good few weeks before that plaster cast comes off. It's really kind of you to have a meal waiting. I'll be as quick as I can.'

'You take your time. Nothing's spoiling. By the way, you know you could have asked me to come back to Manchester for these. I'm very well used to driving back and forth, you know. And I love driving my new Mercedes.'

'Yes, I know, but you'd only just left a few days ago and I didn't think it was fair.' James had dashed back to Dornoch to oversee the production line.

'You are so kind and sweet, Sarah.'

'I had an ulterior motive: I wanted to see more of this beautiful country of yours.'

'What a fantastic idea. Can you stay a few days?'

'Yes, I think so. I did bring an overnight bag.'

SICILIAN SUNSET

*

Sarah dragged her weary body up the stairs to the room she had previously occupied. The shower was just what she needed and she felt much better after it. She put on some fresh clothes and went downstairs.

The meal was a refreshing prawn salad, washed down with a crisp white wine. Then James dug some ice cream out of the freezer. Perfect after a hot and sticky day on the road. She felt really tired though and it was obvious to James because straight after the meal he sent her to bed.

The following morning she slept late and it was eleven o'clock when she finally made it into the kitchen. The house was silent. James must have gone to the factory. There was a note stuck on the fridge door. She read the note out loud to herself. 'Had to go out. Some climbers are stuck up a hill. One of them has a broken leg.' Sarah couldn't understand what it meant. What on earth had an emergency like this got to do with James? Sarah toasted some bread and made a cup of tea. Then she walked the short distance to Elizabeth's house.

Elizabeth wasn't her usual friendly self and Sarah could only think it was something to do with the loss of the Mercedes, but she decided not to enquire.

'Do you know where James has gone?'

'Yes. He pushed a note through my door. He's gone out to rescue a climber with a broken leg. The man's been out all night. I think James will have left about four o'clock this morning. He'll want to be getting up that hill as soon as it's light.'

'But why should James have to go?'

'Because, my dear, when he's at home, he always goes out with the rescue services. His army training means he has a lot of experience. Mind you, I'm always worried, although he should be all right today.'

'What d'you mean? You're always worried?' Sarah felt the icy hand of fear squeezing the air from her lungs.

'Well, sometimes the terrain can be very dangerous. One false move and you can plunge hundreds of feet to your death.'

Sarah thought she was going to be sick.

At last Elizabeth took pity on her. 'Sit down, Sarah, before you fall down. Like I said, James should be all right today. He's only going up Ben Klibreck. Mind you, it is over three thousand feet high, but it's a very easy climb if you know what you're doing. The trouble is the poor laddie who's injured has been out all night. One of the other climbers phoned the emergency services yesterday about seven o'clock. But shortly after the party was located a thick mist came down and they couldn't get a helicopter out to them. And he's stuck on a part of the hill where they can't land so I am afraid they will just have to drop our boys as close as possible and then they'll have to walk the rest of the way. And coming back they'll be carrying the man on a stretcher, which makes the job even harder. But I don't doubt for one minute that they'll get him back.'

Sarah decided she'd better return to his house and wait for him there. Elizabeth didn't offer her a cup of tea. In fact she seemed pleased when Sarah left.

She sat waiting for him all day, getting more and more agitated as the hours passed. Suppose something awful happened to him. He'd been so supportive and she'd repaid his kindness by being aloof. She hadn't let him get near her. He was a lovely person and she knew if she hadn't met Tony she would have most likely married James. And what a wonderful husband he would have been. He wouldn't have run away with another woman. What a fool she'd been.

Sarah had just about convinced herself that he was dead when she saw a big rescue vehicle pull up outside. James leapt out looking remarkably fit and agile for someone who had been up a mountain for twelve hours. She flew to the door, opened it and threw herself into his arms.

'What the—'

She silenced him with her lips.

He returned her kiss with equal passion.

She pressed herself up to him, wrapping her arms around his neck and running her fingers through his hair. The kiss went on for an eternity and she felt a tingling sensation run through her body. She knew exactly what she wanted and there was no going back. She broke away from him and, with tears in her eyes, whispered, 'I thought I'd lost you. I thought you were dead.'

'What? Oh Sarah, don't be daft. I was only up a hill.'

'Your mother said it's over three thousand feet high.'

'Come inside, Sarah, and I'll explain at what point a hill becomes a mountain.'

She knew he was teasing her.

'I'm sorry you were scared but on the other hand. . . .' He leaned back on the door to close it and then he pulled her back into his arms.

Sarah was breathless with desire as his mouth covered hers once more.

He pushed her away yet again. 'I must phone Mother on the landline and let her know everything went OK, although she is well used to my little rescue trips. I didn't phone her on my mobile; I only use it in an emergency.' He took off his parka and hung it up. Then he went to the phone and spoke to his mother. 'We got the poor bloke. He was in a lot of pain but by now he'll be in Raigmore.' He listened for a moment. 'Yes. She's here. She's OK. What did you say to her?' He smiled at her reply. Then he put the phone back on its cradle and turned round and walked towards her.

'Mother shouldn't have told you it was dangerous. Sometimes she exaggerates. She seems to think you were concerned for my safety. Are you sure you aren't getting carried away by the moment? I don't want to take advantage of you just because you thought I was in danger. You might regret this tomorrow. I feel obliged to tell you this won't be just a mad fling for me. I missed the boat last time and I don't want to miss it again. We were always well matched. I want you, Sarah. And I want you to marry me.'

Sarah felt slightly worried as she saw the look in his eyes. She could see how serious James was. The look made her analyse her own feelings for him. She knew if this wasn't love, it would be wrong to lead him on. But she felt so happy, it was like being born again. This must be real love, not like she had felt for Tony. She was at last going to be blessed with a man who really loved her. She trusted James. Surely that was the important thing. And marriage was what he wanted because he was an honourable man.

'Sarah.' James looked worried. 'Please speak to me. Tell me I'm on the right track. Please don't tell me I've got it all wrong.'

But still Sarah hesitated. James wanted a real commitment from her. She hoped she wasn't making another mistake. It was such a temptation and she knew they would be good together. But was it right to let him make love to her when he so obviously wanted to marry her and she didn't want to marry him? Yet this might be her last chance; her only chance to be happy. Wouldn't it be insane to sacrifice this chance just because she wasn't madly in love with him? In any case, look where mad passion had got her last time. And didn't everyone say that love was always better, the second time around? Well, this would be the third time around. Suddenly she made up her mind that she wasn't going to blow it either.

'Sarah. Sarah. Please speak to me.'

He was so close now. She noticed a few lines on his forehead. Worry lines or maybe squinting in the Australian sunshine had caused them. Her attention shifted and she gazed into his deep-brown eyes. How could she disappoint him? And let's face it, she did love him. He had always been kind to her. He looked so nervous. At last she found her voice. 'Yes, please, James. I would love to marry you.' There! It was said. The deed was done. She felt safe with James. She knew he would never let her down.

James cupped her face in his hands and covered it with kisses. 'Come upstairs with me, Sarah. I've been waiting for this moment for quite a long time. Four months to be exact, but it seems more like four years.'

Her heart was thumping as he closed the bedroom door. This was silly. She knew she couldn't possibly be nervous. After all, she and James had made love plenty of times. But suppose he didn't find her attractive once he got her into bed? The thought was almost too awful to contemplate but she was after all, forty now. Apart from James and Tony she hadn't had much experience with men. First of all, she'd always been too busy building up her business and secondly she didn't believe in sleeping around. In fact, she had only been to bed with two men: James and Tony.

She'd met James on a design course. He was trying to get a grip on Sutherland Silver. His father had just died and left it jointly to James and Elizabeth. Sarah was at college to get a good grounding on everything to do with setting up a new business. She'd chosen the name Baubles Bangles and Beads and she was renting a market stall. Then she started seeing James. She had been going out with him a couple of years when he asked her to marry him. She'd turned him down because she wasn't ready to give up her independence. And so they'd drifted apart and then Tony came along. And now here she was back with James, still wondering if they were suited. Surely she couldn't be having second thoughts again? James was looking at her; waiting for a sign. She stared up into those warm brown eyes and she just couldn't help herself. She melted into his arms.

He drew her over to his bed and they sank down on it. She felt a tremor of excitement run through her body as he kissed her lips. She closed her eyes as his fingers traced the outline of her face. Then suddenly he was kissing her neck and unbuttoning her blouse. He eased it from her shoulders and then, unclipping her bra, he pushed her back against the pillows. She let herself be carried away on a wave of pure happiness. The ten years they had spent apart slipped away. He knew exactly what buttons to press.

Wave after wave of pleasure poured over her as he stroked every inch of her skin with a feather-like touch. She gasped with delight as he took his fill of her and then he lavished more attention on her body till she reached the dizzy height of her own primitive desires and had to push him away. 'Wow, James. Was it as good as this ten years ago?'

He smiled down at her. 'No, but I think it was quicker.'

Sarah blushed. 'I think it's much better, slower.'

'So do I my darling. And now you'll have to make an honest man out of me.'

They spent the next day in bed, inflamed with desire and not being able to get enough of one another. Eventually they made their way back downstairs.

Sarah was bubbling with joy. Who should she tell first? Her dad? Jane? Then she felt a slight shiver run through her body. They would have to tell Elizabeth. How would she take it? A few months ago she wouldn't have given it a thought, but lately Elizabeth had been very cool towards her. She was sure it was something to do with the episode over Neil. 'Are we both going to tell your mother, together?'

'Oh for goodness sake! Don't look so scared. I keep telling you, Mother likes you. She's forgotten all about that débâcle over Neil. We'll go over now and tell her. Get it over with and then you'll see I'm right.'

But Sarah didn't feel James was right at all. When they walked hand-in-hand down Elizabeth's garden path she had a premonition that it wouldn't be, as James expected it to be, plain sailing and Sarah was right. Although Elizabeth congratulated them, her eyes remained cold. Why was it, thought Sarah, that men were so blind to all the signs particularly where their mothers were concerned?

'See, I told you it would be fine,' James said, when they were in bed that night.

'I hope it is, but I don't want your mother to know we're sleeping together when we're not married.'

'I admit, you're probably right about that. She does belong to a generation that thought sex before marriage was a crime worse than murder, so I promise we'll be discreet but that doesn't mean we can't enjoy it.' He started to kiss her again.

Sarah felt her passion rise yet again. His hands caressed her body and she shivered in delight. 'Oh James,' she moaned, 'you are such an expert at this.'

Suddenly the jangling tones of the phone brought both of them down to earth.

'Oh my God! Who can it be at this time in the morning?' James flicked the bedside light on and reached for the extension.

Sarah was surprised to see it was two o'clock. They'd been

talking and making love for four hours. She felt guilty and she sat up. Suppose his mother had been taken ill while they were.... She forced herself not to go any further with this appalling notion.

'Yes! Yes! I see. Well I'll get over as soon as I can but I don't know how soon that will be. I've got to sort out some funds at my end, book a flight, pack and all that stuff. I'll get Mother to phone you as soon as I step into a taxi and she can give you the flight details so you can meet me.' He slammed down the phone and swore.

'What's the matter?'

'There's a problem at the New York store. It looks very much like the manager has sloped off with some of our money.'

Sarah gasped. 'How terrible. How much?'

'A great deal.'

'How come no one noticed?'

'Because apparently he managed to hide it with some very crafty accounting. Luckily I always employ an independent firm of auditors to check the accounts every six months; it's especially necessary in a place like America where it's a criminal offence to submit incorrect accounts. Even if it's only by mistake, you can go to prison. At least I've got a chance to put things right before the end of the tax year.'

'How are you going to be able to put it right?'

'By transferring an obscene amount of money from my own personal savings.' James sighed. 'All right. I might as well tell you. It looks like he's got away with about a million dollars, or if you want it in pounds that's about seven hundred thousand.'

Sarah turned white. 'But surely you can't....'

'Don't worry about it, Sarah. I can actually afford it and eventually I might get it back if the police catch up with him.'

'And if they don't?'

'Well, it just means I might have to do on a bit less pension when I'm old and grey. Oh stop looking so agitated. This house is not mortgaged and neither is Mother's. And my needs by then will be very small unless I take on a high maintenance wife.'

Sarah laughed and the tension she'd been feeling eased considerably. 'Luckily for you I'm not high maintenance, however if you need to borrow—'

'Don't even think about it. The worst thing is, I'll have to go over to New York just at the time when life has become so much fun for me. So you'll keep away from the Anderson boy while I'm gone, will you?'

'I could be persuaded—'

He silenced her with a kiss that told her how much he wanted her. She sank back on to the pillows waiting for him to make love to her again, but he didn't.

'That's so you'll remember what it's all about and now we'd better get some sleep. Tomorrow you can help me pack.'

CHAPTER SEVEN

James flew off to the USA two days later so with time on her hands, Sarah decided to phone her father and tell him the exciting news. He was delighted. Sarah was feeling flushed with success at getting her father's approval so she decided to ring Jane, but her reaction wasn't anywhere near as warm as George Simpson's had been.

'Don't you think it's a bit soon for all this?'

'What? What are you talking about? You're the one that tried to push me into a romance with James.'

'I did no such thing.'

'Yes you did. You were the one who called him "tasty" and you went on about men in kilts being sexy.'

'I said romantic not sexy. I well remember what I said and I didn't tell you to get engaged to him.'

'I don't understand. I thought you liked him.' Sarah was close to tears.

'I do like him. I think he's gorgeous and from what I know of him, he's a very nice bloke, but he's been married before and divorced and he's only been back in your life a few months.'

'But I've known him over ten years and we were very close at one time.'

'Yes, and you ditched him for Tony so if he was wrong for

you then, he's wrong for you now.'

'I did not ditch him for Tony. James and I just drifted apart. Anyway what's it got to do with you? I'm fed-up with people trying to manage my life for me. D'you know something? You were always dead bossy at school.' Sarah slammed the phone down.

She had forgotten that she was the one who had phoned Jane. She was smarting from Jane's remarks, but they'd been best friends for thirty years and a best friend had every right to make the comments that Jane had just made. Sarah was suddenly appalled at how she'd just treated her. She picked up the phone and tapped the redial key.

'Jane, don't hang up. I'm sorry. I am truly, truly sorry. I didn't mean what I just said.'

'I know you didn't, sweetie. I was about to call you back. I shouldn't have said the things that I said, either. I was scared that you were jumping in so quickly, but, like you said, you do know James rather well. You're right. You're in love with a very dependable man. Maybe those are the best sort of relationships. Anyway, I wish you both every happiness. You deserve it and you know you can count on me for anything.'

Sarah sighed with relief. She'd had no intention of falling out with Jane like that.

By the time the phone call was over, the two women had aired every topic there was about the forthcoming wedding. They had more or less decided where to get the dress; who to ask to make the cake; suitable honeymoon destinations and even where Sarah might live after she'd married James had been discussed. Sarah was looking forward to getting back to Manchester so they could hit the shops. She felt really upbeat. It was a real shame she didn't notice the big black cloud on the horizon: the one that was about to chuck a hundred gallons of water over her happiness.

*

The doorbell interrupted Sarah's pleasant thoughts about the wedding ceremony. She went to the door and found Elizabeth on the step.

'Oh do come in.' Maybe she's come to apologize for her attitude, thought Sarah. She was willing to give her that chance because she didn't want to get off on the wrong foot with the mother of her husband-to-be. 'Come and sit down. Would you like a cup of tea or coffee, perhaps?'

'No. I really want to get this over as soon as possible.' Elizabeth sounded grim; but she did sit down.

Sarah sat down opposite her and prepared to do battle.

'I think you must have gathered that I wasn't happy at your news.'

Blimey! Sarah thought. She doesn't beat about the bush. 'I didn't think you were very enthusiastic when we told you. I don't understand what I've done; I always used to get on so well with you.'

'It isn't actually anything you have done; it's actually something that James hasn't done. While he was in the SAS—'

Sarah gasped. 'James was in the SAS?'

'Yes, he was, and I thought he'd told you, which makes this whole business even worse. Seeing as James hasn't told you himself I suspect he'll be very angry if he gets to know I've told you. Up until today only his father and I knew. It's been a well-kept secret and I would like it to stay that way. However I'll get back to the main issue. When I said it was something James hasn't done I meant, he hasn't obtained a divorce from his first wife.'

Sarah's heart almost stopped beating. 'No! No! That can't be right,' she blurted out. 'Marilyn would never have married Carlo if she hadn't got a divorce.'

'I'm not talking about Marilyn. As a matter of fact Marilyn was his second wife. I'm talking about his first wife: a woman called Sandra Mason.'

'Who's Sandra Mason?'

'She was a nurse he met while serving in the SAS in Brunei and he married her.'

'No! I don't believe you. Why are you doing this? Do you really hate me so much that you'll say anything to stop me marrying James?'

'My dear, I don't hate you. I have never hated you. I must admit I was a bit surprised by your flighty behaviour. First there was Neil, then Louis and then Maurice.'

Sarah didn't bother to correct her, but it did explain Elizabeth's recent coolness.

'But it's not that. It's something else. Just let me show you.' Elizabeth fished in her bag and pulled out a battered envelope. 'Have a look inside.' She took a small lace handkerchief from the bag and dabbed her eyes with it.

Sarah could hardly bear to look in the envelope, but she needed to know what Elizabeth was going on about. She must have got hold of the wrong end of the stick. Sarah slipped her fingers into the envelope and pulled out a piece of paper. Unfolding it, she looked at it and tried to read the faded words but they were written in a foreign language. There were some words she could make out however. They were names. James Ross and Sandra Mason. She looked up at Elizabeth. 'I can't read it.'

'Neither can I, but it's quite obvious that it's a marriage licence.'

'You can't say that. It could be anything.' Sarah's voice rose. 'This isn't proof that James married this Mason woman.'

'No, but these are,' declared Elizabeth, and with the expertise of a magician, she pulled more envelopes out of her bag and put them into Sarah's lap.

'What are these? These are addressed to James. You can't possibly have read them surely?'

Elizabeth was crying openly now. 'Yes, I have read them and believe me I don't feel good about it but I had to. I just had to. I needed to know the truth. The sender's name was on the back: Sandra Ross.'

Sarah pushed them back into Elizabeth's hands. 'I'm not reading them.'

'Then I'm going to have to tell you what's in them. You need to know. These letters are all about a baby. A baby called Jamie Ross. Sandra's baby. He's seventeen and living with Sandra in America. What I am trying to say is; James has a wife and a son living in Washington. And if he marries you he'll be a bigamist just like he was when he married Marilyn.'

Sarah felt an iron band tighten around her heart. It felt like it had stopped beating. She couldn't breathe. She looked at Elizabeth in horror and watched her face get smaller and smaller till it was no bigger than a tennis ball. And then Sarah fainted.

She came back to her senses to find Elizabeth holding a bottle of smelling salts under her nose. She gasped for air.

'Thank goodness I always carry this old-fashioned remedy around with me. Don't move. I'm going into the kitchen to bring you a glass of water.'

Sarah gulped the water down.

'Steady, my dear. Drink it slowly.'

'I've never fainted before in my life,' Sarah whispered.

'And I feel responsible for that. I know what I told you was a big shock, but I couldn't have told it any differently. What are you going to do?'

'Do? What am I going to do? I'll tell you what I'm going to

do. I'm getting out of here as soon as possible before James gets back.'

'I meant, are you going to the police?'

It suddenly dawned on Sarah that James would probably go to prison over this. She looked into his mother's eyes. Elizabeth looked absolutely terrified.

'I suppose you've kept this a secret? How long have you known?'

'Since December 1990. James was abroad again. He was still in the SAS. I was looking for some deeds to some land that he wanted us to sell. And then I came across the marriage certificate.'

'But that was just before he married Marilyn in 1991. Why didn't you warn her? Why didn't you stop them getting married?'

'Because they got married on Grand Cayman without telling anyone. It seems Marilyn wasn't on very good terms with her family and wanted a quiet wedding somewhere private. More like somewhere posh, if you ask me. I was hurt at the time, but I had a more pressing problem on my mind. That certificate is dated April 1990 and I realized that James wouldn't have had time to get a divorce. I didn't dare say anything to him in case he thought I'd been going through his things. Anyway, I was hoping I was mistaken. I hope you don't go to the police. If you look at in another light, James has now divorced Marilyn so technically speaking he isn't a bigamist anymore.'

Sarah knew that what Elizabeth was saying made sense and what was the point of going to the police? 'All right. I won't go to the police but I'm still leaving.'

'My dear Sarah, I am so very, very sorry it's ended like this.'

'So am I, but you've done the right thing.'

*

Sarah drove back to Manchester as fast as she could, taking only two toilet breaks. She spent the time going over and over all the gory details until her head swam with facts, but she was no nearer to understanding why James had behaved in this way. As soon as she arrived back home she rang Jane to ask if she could see her at once. When Jane opened the door she was in no doubt that something very bad had happened because there were tears streaming down Sarah's face.

'Come inside at once.' Jane took her arm and steered her into the lounge. 'Sit down. What on earth's happened?'

'It's James,' gasped Sarah. 'He's already married.'

'What? No! Never! He can't be!'

'He is but you've got to swear to me that you won't tell a soul. His mother told me everything. It's absolutely ghastly.'

By the time Sarah had given Jane all the details, she was exhausted. 'I need to get away. And I'm going to see Marilyn. She deserves to know the truth.'

'You can't tell her: she'll go to the police.'

'No, she won't. She'll be too frightened of a scandal. She won't want to blacken the Vasari family name. But if James comes looking for me, you mustn't say where I've gone. In fact, don't even tell him I've been here.'

Sarah landed at Fiumicino Airport in Rome and got a taxi almost straight away. She asked the driver to take her to the Palazzo Vasari. Sarah was thankful he didn't ask her where it was because she couldn't remember the name of the road or the district. She only realized on the plane that James had all those details and she'd never asked him for them. So it was a relief that the driver didn't question her. As soon as he heard the name of the villa he set off, driving like a bat out of hell. Eventually he dropped her in a square and pointed to a tree-lined avenue which Sarah recognized. She knew the villa was at the other end and that meant she had to walk about a quarter of a mile. Struggling with her schoolgirl Italian, she tried to get the driver to take her right up to the villa but he got out and held the car door open, gesticulating for her to get out. For some strange reason he seemed scared. She couldn't understand it because the area where Marilyn and Carlo lived was very opulent. She watched him drive off and it reminded her of the last time they were at Carlo's place. That taxi driver had acted in exactly the same way.

She started to walk up the immaculate road. She was turning all the facts over in her mind. What on earth would she say to Marilyn and, more to the point, how could she explain her sudden appearance to Carlo? She had no intention of telling Marilyn about Sandra in front of Carlo, so she'd better get a good story lined up. The sun was shining and it was hot. Sarah was dragging a trolley case and was starting to feel faint with the heat. She didn't notice a man on a scooter was tailing her.

Suddenly he swooped. He grabbed her shoulder bag and pulled, breaking the strap in the process and wrenching her arm almost from its socket. She tried to stop him but he gave her a vicious push and drove off. Sarah fell to the ground, hitting her head on the pavement. She lay where she'd fallen, oblivious to everything and surrounded by a solid black wall of pain.

CHAPTER EIGHT

James arrived back in Dornoch a month after he'd left. He'd been trying to talk to Sarah on the phone all the time he was away, but he kept getting a recorded message. He was worried sick but he didn't dare leave New York until everything had been sorted out. He'd spoken to his mother and she'd told him that Sarah had got a nasty summer cold and couldn't speak on the phone. But Elizabeth's words didn't ring true.

When he found out what his mother had done he was absolutely furious. 'I can't believe that you've done this, Mother.' He was trying not to shout.

'You have no right to take this attitude. If anyone's in the wrong, it's you. You could have gone to prison for what you did.'

'I think you'd better sit down while I tell you the truth instead of some half-baked idea that you've deduced from a document that you can't even read. Actually, why did you tell Sarah everything?'

'Because she's been messing about with Neil and Maurice and—'

'Sarah has been unhappy and confused but it's Tony we should blame.'

By the time James had finished telling his mother the facts she was in tears. 'I'm so sorry. I should have trusted you and Sarah. What on earth are we going to do?'

'You're going to stay here and look after the business while I drive down to Manchester and see her.'

But when James got to Manchester, Sarah wasn't there. Her father said he didn't even know she'd left Dornoch. James knew by his calm expression that he wasn't telling the truth, so he went to see Jane. He could tell from Jane's cagey expression that if anyone was hiding something, it was Sarah's closest friend. But he could also see there was no way he was going to get anything out of her and he had a good idea why. Sarah must have told her he was married. There was nothing for it: he'd have to tell her everything.

After he'd finished telling her the long and complicated tale she was utterly devastated. 'Oh God, James, and you didn't think to tell Sarah all this?'

'I didn't give it a thought. It was in my past and it didn't affect me anymore. And it was tied up with me being in the army. You do know, don't you, you can't tell anyone I've been in the SAS?'

'I do understand. Presumably it will put your life at risk.'

'Maybe and maybe not, but I don't want to take the chance. So now are you going to tell me where Sarah is hiding?'

'I still can't because I don't actually know exactly where she is. But I know where she was heading. She said she was going to Rome to tell Marilyn everything.'

'Oh bloody hell!' James swore loudly. 'Oh God! Sorry, Jane. Oh God! I'm going to have to go after her, but I won't make it before she gets to Marilyn. She's got too much of a head start. She's bound to have told them all by now.'

'Not necessarily. In fact, if you think about it, if she had told them, don't you think Marilyn or Carlo would have been in touch? Let's face it, the fact that you married Sandra affects Marilyn more than Sarah.'

Jane had a point, thought James. Maybe Sarah had changed her mind, but if so why hadn't she come back to England?

'Why don't you phone Marilyn?'

'No. I don't think I should talk about this over the phone. I'll send Sarah a text and tell her my mother—'

'No. You can't do that.'

'Why?'

Jane got up and went to a sideboard. Pulling open the top drawer she held up Sarah's mobile. 'She left this with me.'

'Bloody hell, Jane. Why did you let her do that? Now none of us can phone her.'

'Well, I'm sorry, James. I did tell her she was being stupid, but she was pretty much out of control. I told her she should never be without her mobile in case of emergencies. But she was adamant that she didn't want to hear from you. Actually she threw it across the room just before she dashed out of the door. It was lucky that I caught it before it hit the wall. She has really lost her senses. What are you going to do, James?'

'I'm going to follow her to Rome.'

It took a few days before James could organize his trip to Rome because he'd left Dornoch without a change of clothes so he had to drive the 400 miles back. Then he had to pack and get a flight from Inverness to London and another flight to Rome. So, what with his stint in America, James arrived six weeks after Sarah. But when he went to Carlo's place there was no sign of life and the security officer on the gates told him that Signore and Signora Vasari had taken their children on holiday.

He flew back to Manchester in a state of anxiety mixed with fear. He got a taxi and went to see George Simpson again and this time George took pity on him.

'Look, lad, you can stop worrying about her. She phoned me while you were in New York, but she was in a real state. She said on no account was I to tell you she'd phoned. She rang again last week and she says she's fine and she's taking a much-needed holiday. I'm glad because she hasn't had a holiday since Tony died. I gather you two have had a disagreement.'

'Why d'you say that?' James wondered what Sarah had told her father. Not the truth, apparently, or George wouldn't be being so friendly.

'She's asked me not to tell you where she is. Oh, don't look so embarrassed. This is typical of Sarah. What was it about? I'll stake my life on it being about Living Stones. She's always been obsessive about the company. It's always been her baby and she's got worse since Tony died. So is that it?'

'Yes,' James mumbled, hating himself for lying to George.

'Well, don't worry, son. She'll be back as soon as she's sorted out her priorities. I'll tell you something that should put you out of your misery, she's having a holiday with your ex-wife, Marilyn Vasari.' His eyes twinkled. 'They'll be talking about you.'

Oh yes, thought James, as another taxi drove him to Wytcherley Hall. They'll be talking about me all right. He banged hard on the door, forgetting there was a doorbell.

'James! James! What on earth's happened?' Jane looked terribly anxious.

'Nothing I hope. I've just got back from Rome. There was no one at the Palazzo Vasari.'

'No one?' repeated Jane, ushering him inside.

'No one at all. Not Sarah, Marilyn, and not Carlo. The family had gone on holiday. So I flew back and went to see George and, guess what?'

'What?'

'He's just admitted he had a phone call from her over a month ago.'

'You're joking! What did she say?'

James took off his coat and sat down before replying. 'She hasn't told him anything about me. He thought we'd just had a minor tiff about the business, but she's told him not to tell me where she is.'

'No!'

'Oh yes, but George said it was typical of Sarah, flying off in a huff; he said she'd be back as soon as she's sorted out her priorities.'

'But you don't think she will?'

'No! And actually it bothers me that she thinks I'm a bigamist. I'm going to track her down, or rather I'm going to get a private detective to do the job for me.'

'That's going to cost you a fortune.'

'I don't care. It'll be worth it. I've got to see her so I can put the record straight.'

'Good luck. I hope you find her. So where are you going next?'

'I'm going into Manchester city centre to get the ball rolling. I think I'll go with the bloke I hire and—'

'What? Back to Rome?'

'Yes. I want to be close enough to grab her before she disappears again.'

'Before you go, let me give you a meal and a hot drink because you look as though you could do with a rest.'

'That's very good of you. By the way, have you got a recent photo of her?'

Before he left, Jane made him promise to come back and stay with her till the detective could arrange the trip.

'Face it, James. He won't be able to go at the drop of a hat so you might as well stay here.'

But the detective was having none of it. 'No! Definitely not. I'm sorry, Mr Ross, but I work alone. Completely alone. I'm not having a client hanging on my coat tails, queering my pitch. You have got no idea the dirty tricks I have to perform in order to get information from some people. It can be most embarrassing, not to mention dangerous. But don't worry. This is a legitimate outfit. I submit proper accounts to the taxman. So therefore you will get a proper breakdown of all my expenses. But I go it alone or not at all. I'm the expert in this field.'

James knew that was right. A friend had recommended the agency. So James gave him some advance expenses and Sarah's photo. He went back to Jane's.

'I'm not going.'

'Then you might as well stay here until that fella comes up with the goods. We'll be delighted to have you if can take a break from business.'

'Yes, of course I can. Everything is running smoothly at the moment. It's kind of you to ask me to stay. I'm so worried and at least I can talk to you about Sarah.'

CHAPTER NINE

Sarah might have died by the side of the road if a kind lady from the house opposite hadn't called the ambulance. And then she dashed out with a pillow and a blanket and sat by the unconscious stranger till the ambulance arrived.

She woke up in hospital to find a doctor and nurse leaning over her. 'Where am I?' she whispered.

The doctor raised his eyebrows at the nurse and said something in Italian. Then he spoke haltingly to Sarah. 'You are English?'

'Yes.'

The doctor spoke again in rapid Italian and the nurse left the room. He then took Sarah's temperature and placed a soothing hand on her forehead.

Sarah suddenly realized how queasy she felt.

The door opened and the nurse came back followed by another one. 'Hello.' The second nurse took hold of Sarah's hand. 'Are you from England?'

'Yes.'

'I speak good English. I spend five years in London so please tell us your name and where we can contact your family.'

'What's happened to me?'

'You were involved in an accident. A man snatched your bag and pushed you to the ground. A lady living opposite saw it all. She called an ambulance. But because your bag was stolen we didn't know who you were. The thief left the case with all your clothes but we now need to contact whoever was with you in Rome.'

'I'm not with anyone. I came to visit my friend Marilyn Vasari. I was on my way to the Palazzo Vasari. Please can you phone her for me?' Even though Sarah still felt woozy she couldn't fail to notice the looks that the doctor and nurses exchanged. What the hell is wrong with everyone today? 'Please can you tell me the date?'

'It is the fourth of June,' answered the nurse. 'You've been unconscious for two days. Do not worry. We will contact your friend. Now we must take you down for another scan and some tests, but I will stay by your side.'

Sarah was exhausted from the tests and was dozing when the door opened and Marilyn rushed in with Carlo following close behind her.

'Oh my God. We could hardly believe the doctor when he said you were asking for us. But it *is* you. Whatever are you doing here in Rome and in hospital? Where is James?'

'In America, I think. Please, Marilyn, will you take me to the embassy? I have no money and no papers.'

'Yes. The doctor told us what had happened. We are so sorry that this should happen in our country. It is, unfortunately, a sign of the times. But you can't just go to the embassy. You must come back with us to our home. Carlo will arrange everything. He will ask the doctor if you can be discharged and he will go and see someone at the embassy and see if we can get you a duplicate passport. Then we'll phone James.'

'No!' Sarah gasped in a panic. 'Please don't phone James. I

don't want him to know I'm here.'

Carlo and Marilyn looked bewildered at this request, but Sarah was getting very distressed so they didn't argue with her.

Within a couple of hours of waking up, Sarah was lying on a bed in the Palazzo Vasari. Carlo had brought her trolley case and then he'd gone off to the British Embassy. Sarah was still feeling sick, but she knew she didn't have much time to put Marilyn in the picture before Carlo came back. Marilyn was absolutely appalled but she promised not to tell Carlo the whole story.

'He's going to come looking for me,' whispered Sarah, her eyes wide with fear, 'and I don't want to see him, ever again.'

'Then you shan't,' Marilyn declared, 'at least not until you're ready to face him. In fact, we'll face him together. There are quite a number of things I want to say to that man. But for now, we'll get you out of Rome. We have a small villa on Sicily. We'll all go there. It's extremely well protected and James will never find you.'

Marilyn was true to her word. The following day they all flew out on Carlo's private jet, from Rome's Ciampino Airport and within the hour they were landing at Palermo.

'It's only about an hour's drive to our villa in Cefalu. You will love it. You must stay as long as you want. It's so nice for me to have an English friend as a guest. I do sometimes miss living in England, you know. You look so tired, Sarah. Why don't you have a little nap? It's nice and peaceful with our children travelling in the other car.'

Sarah regretfully let her eyes close. She would have loved to see her first glimpse of Sicily but Marilyn was right: she felt like death warmed up.

It seemed only minutes before Marilyn gently woke her up. 'We're here.'

They swept through some massive black, cast-iron gates and up a long winding drive, past beautifully manicured lawns that looked like they were regularly watered. Villa Vallerina was a sprawling white building, all on one level. Sarah could see a deep blue infinity pool overlooking the aquamarine Mediterranean. As she followed Marilyn into the cool villa and through an inner courtyard she felt instantly refreshed. Someone had placed lush green palms in honey-coloured planters and they swayed gently in the cool breeze that wafted though the building. All the floors were cream marble and they also helped to keep the villa nicely chilled.

'Here we are. These are your rooms.'

The beauty of the sitting-room overwhelmed Sarah. Then she glanced through the window and exclaimed with delight, 'What a fabulous view.' She could see the sun dropping behind the distant mountains. It was the most vibrant sunset she had ever seen. The mountains formed an inky black line against a burnt ochre sky dappled with the last pale turquoise remnants of a perfect summer's day. She wanted to gaze at it forever.

'I thought you would be happier on this side of the villa. You haven't got a view of the pool or the sea but trust me, if you heard our children playing in the pool in the early hours of the morning you'd know why we put our guests here. These rooms face west and the sun doesn't get round here till late afternoon so it will be nice and cool for you as well. Anyway, come and have a look at the bedroom and the bathroom.'

'This is so gorgeous.' The bedroom walls were natural beige sandstone and there were hessian curtains at the windows. She touched them and her senses were inundated with the warm Mediterranean smell of lemons, Ambre Solaire and salt water. Suddenly and inexplicably, it reminded her of Mallorca and the tears sprang into her eyes.

'Please don't cry, Sarah.' Marilyn hugged her. 'I know you must be tired. You slip into bed and have a nice sleep. I'll get Maria to come and wake you and I'll make sure it's in plenty of time, so you can have a shower before dinner.'

Sarah did as she was told and when Maria finally came to wake her, she felt much better. 'What a wimp I am,' she told herself whilst she was in the shower. 'I'm going to have to stop feeling sorry for myself.' She was just towelling herself down when there was another knock at the door. Must be Marilyn, she thought. She wrapped the bath sheet around herself, went to the door and opened it.

A man was lounging against the wall by the door. He had a glorious tan and designer sunglasses were perched on top of his head. His hair was spiked with gel but he'd failed to control the tangle of jet-black curls. His smile was warm and infectious. Sarah looked into his sparkling eyes. It was like looking into the blue waters of a crystalline pool. She felt like she was drowning. He was absolutely drop-dead gorgeous.

Sarah was hypnotized. The towel slipped from fingers that suddenly had no feeling in them. The man quickly averted his eyes, bent down, grabbed the towel and held it up in front of her, effectively shielding her. Her face was red as a beetroot. He leaned towards her and with infinite care he gently wrapped the bath sheet around her naked body.

'Marilyn says dinner is ready' He had a slight American accent.

A whisper of cedar and patchouli washed over her. It was his clean ocean-fresh cologne. She closed her eyes and inhaled. Good God! What the hell was she doing? She opened her eyes to see him walking away. What on earth must he have thought of her? Well, it was no good worrying. He was obviously a servant and she probably wouldn't see him again.

Maria had told her that while she was asleep, Marilyn had filled the wardrobe with designer dresses. 'She told me to tell you, Carlo is always buying her something new. The dress shops all know her size. But she never gets round to wearing them all.'

She picked out a pale-green chiffon dress that she knew was way out of her financial league. The pure silk underskirt was a deep peacock blue. She knew she'd chosen it because it reminded her of the iridescent turquoise and green waters round Scotland's east coast. The pretty creation floated round her legs like a delicate dream.

As she walked along through the courtyard she caught a movement through an open door. It was Marilyn. Sarah stopped, but before she could step into the room she saw a man. She watched Marilyn throw her arms around his neck and they exchanged a passionate kiss. As they drew apart, Sarah was horrified to see that it was the servant she'd just found outside her door. She pulled back and walked quickly in the opposite direction but she wasn't fast enough.

'Sarah! Sarah!' Marilyn called. 'Hang on, wait a minute. You're going the wrong way. Salvatore will show you to the dining-room.'

Sarah turned round reluctantly. She was startled to see the man's arm was still around Marilyn's waist. They certainly weren't trying to hide anything.

Suddenly Carlo popped his head round the door. 'Sarah come and meet my brother, Salvatore.'

Sarah walked slowly towards them.

'We've already met,' said Salvatore, as he linked arms with her. 'Come this way, please.' He took her into the dining-room.

Sarah could hear children's voices drawing nearer but she was still alone with Salvatore Vasari and her legs had just turned to jelly. She almost collapsed into the chair that he pulled out for her.

He bent down and whispered, 'Don't worry, Sarah, I didn't see anything.'

Dinner was a wonderful affair for Sarah who had missed out on family life for so long. Being an only child had been lonely. Then she'd married Tony but they'd been too busy to have children. Probably a good thing in view of what had happened, she thought to herself. Then she chided herself for getting maudlin yet again. The children had elected to speak in English and she knew it was to make her feel at home. Salvatore had very quickly slipped into the seat next to her and Sarah found herself enjoying his company.

Apparently he'd been away in America for ten years running the family business, but he didn't say what it was and she felt it would be rude to ask. He was thirty-five which was five years younger than Sarah but she couldn't care less. The two brothers looked very much alike. They both had the same disarming smiles set in broad, sun-tanned faces, but Carlo was the elder by three years.

Salvatore told her there were four sisters and two more brothers. 'Donatello is thirty and Michelo is twenty-eight. But you have no need to bother about them, Sarah, because they are both married. But I'm not married so we can, as you English put it so nicely, hang out together. Yes?'

'Yes,' she agreed weakly, giggling. She saw Marilyn smiling at them across the table. It was obvious she was delighted that Salvatore and Sarah had hit it off and she made a point of telling her so later that evening as she walked Sarah to her bedroom.

'I'm so pleased you like Salvatore. He's a wonderful man. He's so kind and thoughtful. He's brought me a beautiful necklace back from New York. See.' She touched the tiny diamonds that lay like confetti around her neck. The thin gold chains that supported them were hardly visible and it looked as though the diamonds had just been sprinkled on to her skin.

Sarah was thankful that she knew it wasn't from James's shop because Sutherland Silver didn't do diamonds. 'That is really gorgeous but. . . .'

'I know what you're going to say: you're wondering what Carlo thinks.'

'Mmm! Yes. I'm sorry. It's not any of my business.'

'You saw me kissing him, didn't you?'

Sarah sighed. She didn't want to get involved. She looked down at the floor. A peal of laughter from Marilyn made her look up.

'You have no idea about the Italians, have you? They are so generous and so demonstrative. Everybody kisses everybody and it's never just a peck on the cheek. It's always a full-blown whopper on the mouth except they don't—'

'Marilyn!' Sarah screamed, 'Don't you dare tell me any more.' Then she started laughing. 'How do you stand it? Suppose it's someone dead gross?'

'You just have to keep your eyes peeled, and if he looks like Quasimodo you just have to keep on the move. But if it's someone like Salvatore, well, I say just lean back and enjoy it and you will if he kisses you. Mark my words, Sarah. He is the most delicious kisser I know. Possibly better than his brother,' she mused.

'Which one?' giggled Sarah.

'All of them,' laughed Marilyn.

The two women collapsed on Sarah's bed. Tears of laughter

were rolling from Sarah's eyes. It was the first time she had felt so happy for ages. 'So they've all kissed you, have they?'

'Of course they have. And it's always enjoyable when they do.' Marilyn screamed with laughter and then hugged her, 'Listen, Sarah, I want you to enjoy yourself while you're here. I want you to forget all about James. Salvatore is a lovely person. He's a real gentleman. He won't do anything that you don't want him to. But if you want to go anywhere you should ask him to take you. You will be safe with him.'

'What do you mean? Safe?' Sarah wrinkled her brows in puzzlement.

'You won't have noticed yet, but there are a good few men all around the villa and its gardens.'

'Yes I know. Servants. You must be very rich to have—'

'Not servants, Sarah. Bodyguards.'

'Bodyguards!' Sarah was horrified.

'Not just bodyguards; actually they are all members of Carlo's family. Admittedly some of them are only cousins many times removed, but that's what Sicilia is like. All families stick together. It's not entirely safe to roam the streets on your own. You know what happened in Rome; well, it can happen here, so please don't leave the confines of the villa alone. Anyway, I must go and see to the children. As it's Saturday tomorrow, they were allowed to stay up much later tonight than usual and they'll need settling down. Perhaps you'd like to relax by the pool tomorrow?'

CHAPTER TEN

The following morning she asked Marilyn if she could use the landline because she'd left her mobile with Jane. She told her why she'd left it. Marilyn patted her arm and told her it was a good job she'd left it behind, because otherwise it would have been in the bag that had been stolen. Sarah wanted to phone her father. She knew when James told him that she'd shot off on her own, he'd be worried.

'Hi Dad. I've got a little surprise for you. I'm not in Dornoch.' She knew she had to lie. 'I'm in Rome. Well, you've been on at me for months to have a holiday. But listen. On absolutely no account must you tell James where I am.' She could tell by the silence, at the other end of the phone, that her father was puzzled. 'He's in New York, on business. We've had a terrible row and I don't want to see him. Please, Dad. He'll only try and bully me into coming back.'

Her father wasn't keen on keeping secrets from James, but in the end he agreed to do it. She knew that once he'd promised not to tell James, he wouldn't. She did tell him that she was with Marilyn so he knew she was perfectly safe. After the phone call she put on a loose cotton blouse and some shorts and went out in the garden to idle her time away. The hit and run had taken more out of her than she knew and suddenly she was asleep.

She awakened to find herself in the shade of a large umbrella with Salvatore sitting opposite her, watching her.

'Is good thing I came out here. You were right in the sun. You could have been severely burnt. I bring you this umbrella. You have been asleep for two hours.'

'Oh no!' Sarah gasped.

'Sarah! Sarah! Don't worry. Is all right. Your accident has made you want to sleep and is good that you get proper rest. You will recover much quicker. But I think you should go and change and then you can have a refreshing swim. Carlo and Marilyn have taken the children out and we will have the pool all to ourselves.'

Sarah noticed he had a pair of tight black shorts under a white, short-sleeved shirt. He looked ready for a swim but she hesitated. What was she getting into?

'Marilyn has put some bikinis in your room. She told me to tell you they are new and she hasn't worn them. She said you are to take your pick.'

Oh to hell with it, Sarah thought. I'm going to enjoy myself. She went into the house and tried on the three bikinis. In the end she decided on the more modest of the three. It had a cropped top and shorts that she could easily have worn to a game of tennis. She didn't want to show too much flesh especially after the previous night.

When she returned to the pool, Salvatore was waiting with a bottle of suntan lotion in his hand. 'Come here, Sarah. I think we should spray you all over with this. This is waterproof and it will protect you in the pool, but as soon as you get out you must cover up. The sun is very strong here in Sicily and I don't want you to burn.'

'I've already put some suntan lotion on.'

'Maybe it is not enough. Here the air is very clear and the

sun's rays very strong. Stronger than you English are used to.'

Sarah screamed when the cold spray hit her skin, but she knew Salvatore was right about the sun. Marilyn had said he was kind and thoughtful and he was.

'And I also have something special for the nose.' He had a stick of solid sunblock in his hand and he grabbed her shoulders. 'Stand still, Sarah.'

She was dying to look into his eyes but instead she looked at his mouth. His lips turned up slightly at the corners even when he wasn't smiling, like now, when he was concentrating. There was a faint hint of stubble around them. He was carefully painting the block on her nose. She was so close to him. His lips looked enticingly soft. He smiled at her and she felt an unexpected desire to trace his smile with her finger, but instead she looked up into his eyes and once again she experienced the sensation of drowning. She laughingly pushed him away.

'Thank you very much. I think I am now extremely well protected from the sun.'

They swam up and down, racing one another and laughing. Then they tried to duck one another. Sarah could see Salvatore was surprised that she was such a strong swimmer.

'Sarah. I must rest. You have shattered me.' He climbed out of the pool and leaned down to grasp her hand.

Shattered or not, he lifted her with confident ease and suddenly she was out of the water and standing right in front of him. His sun-hot body was close to hers and she knew instinctively that he wanted to kiss her. But she sensed he was wary. He didn't want to take advantage of her. She stared into his eyes without moving. Maybe if she didn't move away he would kiss her and, oh, how she wanted him to kiss her.

'Sarah,' he whispered. 'You must know I want to. . . .'

She put a hand behind his head and stood slightly on tiptoe.

He was satisfied with the answer and his mouth covered hers, soft but strong.

Sarah felt her heart miss a beat as her mouth opened like a rose caressed by the sun. Her senses exploded into a honey-flavoured dream. She swayed towards him. She had no control of her body. If he let go of her now she knew she would fall back into the pool. But he didn't. He pulled her even closer.

Finally the kiss ended but Salvatore still held her in his arms. Then he took her hand to lead her into the house.

'No. I can't. It's too soon.'

He misunderstood. 'Ah *cara mia*. Your head. It still hurts you. No matter. We will wait. And maybe is good you say no because Carlo and Marilyn are back with the children.'

'I think I'll go and have a shower,' Sarah muttered.

'Me too, but mine will have to be a cold one.' He smiled at her laughter.

Sarah knew he wasn't annoyed with her. Some men might have tried to push her to go further or branded her with a particular label, but not Salvatore. He was happy to wait till she was ready. The trouble was, the awful way Tony had left her and the cruel way James had deceived her might mean that she would never be ready.

Dinner could have been awkward with another man but Salvatore treated her exactly as he had the night before. Nevertheless, Sarah felt she owed him an explanation and as soon as she could pluck up the courage she needed, she would tell him everything. But first she had to find out how much Marilyn had told Carlo. She resolved to tackle Marilyn after dinner.

The two women were in Sarah's sitting-room.

'You wanted to talk to me?'

'Yes. I was wondering what you've told Carlo about James.'

'Nothing as yet. I was waiting to get the go-ahead from you. Why?'

'I want to tell Salvatore.'

'Wow! He's made a move on you already, hasn't he? Come on! Give!'

Sarah blushed as crimson as the setting sun. 'Well. Not really.'

'Not really? What does that mean? Has he kissed you? Wow! He's kissed you.'

Sarah started to laugh. 'Yes,' she admitted.

'What did you think? No! Don't bother to tell me. I can see it all in your face. You loved it, didn't you?'

Sarah blushed even deeper as she remembered how much she had loved it. But then she remembered how it had ended and her eyes filled with tears. 'I can't stop thinking about what James did.'

'Salvatore isn't a bit like James. He's a Sicilian. Honour is everything to a Sicilian. He won't do what James did. You just have to trust him. And I will tell you something: Salvatore has been out with plenty of women, but I have never seen him as happy as this. I think he has fallen in love with you and it's been love at first sight.'

'What should I do?'

'I think we should go to Carlo and you should tell him all about James. He will be furious at the way I've been treated. The thing I am worried about is how he will see it from the family's perspective. I've brought shame and dishonour to his family. He will not be happy about that. I think it may change his feelings towards me.'

'Oh no! Surely not? He adores you.'

But Marilyn still looked worried. 'We should go and tell him now. Get it over with and then let him sleep on it.'

So they went to find Carlo together.

Carlo listened to the story quietly but Sarah knew he was seething. His eyes were angry and his fists were clenched.

By the time Marilyn had finished, both women were in tears.

'Please don't cry. Neither of you is responsible for James and his past. I could have him dealt with, if that's what you want, Sarah?'

'What d'you mean? Dealt with?' Sarah asked, wondering if he was thinking of giving James a black eye or something similar. She was worried; Carlo didn't realize he wouldn't stand a chance against James. The one thing she hadn't told Carlo or Marilyn was that James had been in the SAS and could look after himself very well.

'I have people at my disposal who could have him terminated in the blink of an eye. Do you wish me to do that? If so, Sarah, you only have to say.'

Marilyn was staring at her husband in horror.

My God! Sarah was appalled. 'No! No!' she stammered. 'I just never want to see him again.'

'That will have its difficulties since you work together.'

'I'm leaving the business.' She'd said it without thinking but as soon as she'd said it she realized what a great idea it was.

Marilyn had now switched her attention to Sarah. It was obvious that she was dumbfounded by what Sarah had just said.

'Well, if I can't do anything about James I can at least offer you the sanctuary of our villa for as long as you need it. James will never find you here. As for our position, Marilyn, since you are no longer married to James you have nothing to worry about. Come here, *cara mia.*' He took her into his arms and kissed the top of her head, just as though he was comforting one of his children. Then he murmured something in Italian to her and Marilyn smiled up at him.

Sarah decided it was time to leave them alone so she went back to her rooms. She knew that if she had really fallen in love with Salvatore she would also have to tell him about James and about Tony as well.

A few days later she was sitting in the garden when Salvatore pounced on her. 'Good. I am glad I catch you alone. There is a place I want to show you while the children are at school. It is not somewhere the children can go. It is very dangerous.'

Sarah was mystified and followed Salvatore to the bottom of the garden. It was about a hundred yards long. There was a cast-iron fence and gate that was padlocked. Salvatore produced a key and unlocked it. Then he led her down about twenty stone steps to a terrace surrounded by rose bushes. He took her hand and pulled her over to a two-foot stone wall. 'This is one of the most spectacular views that you can see from this villa. Look down there. That is Cefalu.' He pronounced the first two letters like the English 'ch' in the word church but with a much softer sound. It was exactly how Marilyn had pronounced the middle letters when she called her island, Sicilia. It was a pleasant Italian sound. 'And that is the Tyrrhenian Sea.'

So she'd been wrong to think this was the Mediterranean. The town stretched lazily along several beaches. The bright blue waters of the bay washed up on the yellow sand. And it was all overlooked by a towering granite headland.

'That cliff is absolutely massive,' she whispered in awe.

'That is La Rocca,' replied Salvatore.

Ah! How original, Sarah thought to herself, and giggled.

'What are you laughing at?' Salvatore demanded.

'Mm! Nothing. Just the name. That's all.'

'You think we could have used our imaginations and given it a better name? Possibly so. Is two hundred metres high.'

Sarah did the calculation in her head. Well over 600 feet.

'I think you won't want to laugh at this.' He half-lifted her and half-pushed her on to the low wall.

For one awful moment Sarah thought he was going to throw her over.

'Do not be afraid. I will not let you fall. But you must look down below the wall and tell me how funny that is.'

Sarah peered over the wall and gasped with amazement. It was a sheer drop of about a hundred feet to the sea below. The waves crashed against the jagged rocks on either side but exactly below the wall, the sea disappeared under the cliff.

'This is something that you English call a leap of love, I think?'

Sarah looked puzzled. 'You mean a leap of faith?'

'No. *Amore*. For love. They jump together. Down there, into the sea.'

Light was beginning to dawn. 'You mean a lovers' leap?'

'That is it. That is right. We have great many vendettas on this island in the past. To marry into the wrong family is impossible so from time to time, men and women in love have jumped down into that pool. Gone for good because there is no end to it.'

'You mean it's bottomless,' whispered Sarah. She was horrified at the thought of two young lovers leaping to their deaths on such a beautiful island. But she knew there were places like this in Britain. There was a Lovers' Leap somewhere in the Peak District and then there was the Soldier's Leap in the Pass of Killiecrankie. Strictly speaking it wasn't a Lovers' Leap because the soldier who had jumped, didn't fall to his death. He was merely trying to escape from the Royalists and he chose the narrowest part of the gorge to jump over the River Garry. And he made it.

'Not to worry, *cara mia*. No one has jumped for a long time.'

'How long?'

'At least not since the 1960s and, as this place is now part of our home, it will not happen again because the Vasari family do not have the vendettas any more. Is beautiful spot? Yes?' He pulled her back from the wall. 'Maybe tomorrow I take you down to those beaches and to the harbour of Cefalu. But now we sit down.' He took her hand and guided her to two chairs on either side of a table, obviously meant for lovers to meet and talk.

Sarah knew she wouldn't find a better place or a more opportune moment. So there in the rose-filled arbour she told him everything from the very beginning, thus giving him the chance to dump her. And all the time she was telling him, he never spoke and he never took his eyes off her. And she felt her heart grow colder and colder.

There. It was done. Sarah closed her eyes at the horror of it all and she kept them closed as she heard the metal chair legs scrape along the stone patio. She knew that he was leaving and she knew that when she opened her eyes he would be gone. She opened her eyes. He was gone. She was alone. She bent her head and her tears splashed on to the table. Then the miracle happened as she felt his arms encircle her because he hadn't gone. He was behind her. He took hold of her hands and pulled her up. Once more he wrapped his arms tight about her slim figure. He wasn't much taller than she was but he had enormous strength in his arms.

'*Cara mia*. It mean, my darling. This is what I will always call you. I don't care what has happened to you in the past. It is over. Done with. I love you. Maybe when you know me better you will trust me enough to give me the right answer to the question I will one day ask you. But not now. Not today.'

He bent his head, and as she melted into his arms, his kiss told her he was sincere. Maybe it wouldn't be too long before she could trust him enough to. . . . Her heart pounded as she thought about making love to Salvatore. She had an idea that underneath his cool restraint there was a fiery Sicilian waiting to be set free. She could imagine what it would be like once the door to his cell was unlocked.

CHAPTER ELEVEN

John Parker phoned James on 30 July. He was an ex-policeman and he prided himself on being very, very good at finding missing people. He enjoyed it better than spying on errant husbands or wives because usually missing people were quite happy to be found and reuniting them with their families was very satisfying. It was only ten days since he'd accepted the job from James.

'That was the private detective.'

'Oh my God.' Jane looked apprehensive. 'Has he found her?'

'He wouldn't say. Said he doesn't discuss cases on the phone, but it also seems that he doesn't want to discuss it in his office. He asked me to meet him outside the Town Hall in Albert Square.'

'Albert Square? That's weird. I'll take you.'

'I really appreciate it, but maybe you'd better stay in the car. I got the impression that it's all a bit cloak and dagger. He didn't seem a dramatic sort of bloke though, when I met him,' James said, thoughtfully.

So here he was feeling like Michael Caine, sitting on a bench in Albert Square, Manchester, waiting for a private dick. At least that's what they called them in the films, he mused, smiling to himself. Then suddenly it didn't seem funny. Suppose Sarah was dead. Don't be daft, he told himself. She phoned her father. Remember!

'Good morning, Mr Ross. No! Please don't look at me. Just pretend you don't know me. I've just come to eat a sandwich.' True to his word, he took a sealed plastic pyramid out of his raincoat pocket.

This is really weird, James thought. There was no sign of his briefcase so it looked like he didn't have much to report. James felt his spirits sinking in disappointment. 'I take it you haven't found her.'

'No, I haven't, and I wish you'd told me the sort of people she's mixed up with, because if you had, I wouldn't have taken the job.'

'What the hell do you mean? What sort of people?'

'Don't tell me you didn't know. That Vasari bloke is part of the Mafia and if your little girlie is mixed up with them take my advice: drop her like a hot potato.'

James leaned back against the hard wooden bench. 'No! I don't believe you.'

'I'm telling you. I traced the taxi driver who picked her up at the airport. He didn't want to talk at all. In fact, I had to tempt him with the equivalent of five hundred pounds before he'd open his mouth. Everybody in Rome knows the Palazzo Vasari and who lives there. The taxi driver told me he dropped her at the end of the road. Wouldn't go near the place even though she tried to persuade him.'

James felt like he'd been hit with a baseball bat. He slumped in his seat.

'Our deal's off mate. I don't want to know.' The detective stood up.

'What about your invoice? What about the five hundred pounds?'

'Forget it.' John Parker bent down and pretended to tie his shoelace. 'I pride myself on being able to find anyone. This is the first time I've failed, but I think I'm lucky to be alive. I don't want any dealings with you. Case closed! No further charge!'

James watched him walk casually away. He was aghast by what he'd heard. He hurried back to the car and told Jane. '. . . and he was bloody scared.'

They sat in silence for a while.

'What are you going to do, James?'

'I'm damn well not giving up, that's for sure. If that sod won't work for me I'll go back to Rome on my own and confront Carlo myself.'

'No, you won't go on your own.'

'You're not coming with me; you can forget that.'

'I don't want to come, but you can take Mark. He's just been injured, broken finger, and he's hanging round the house like a lovesick puppy and I don't mean he's lovesick for Pam either. God! I don't know what's wrong with these sportsmen. They simply can't live if they aren't playing their game.'

'Are you sure he'll want to come?'

'Positive; you'll have to tell him everything, but we mustn't tell Pam. I don't want her getting involved.'

'How will she feel about Mark coming to Rome?'

'She'll be ecstatic. He's getting on everyone's nerves, hers included.'

Jane was right. Mark was delighted and so was everyone else.

'They all breathed a sigh of relief when we got in the taxi, you know. Didn't you hear them?'

James laughed. 'I gather you've been putting them through it a bit.'

'Yeah! I've been making their lives hell. Can't help it. Hate being off the team.'

'I'm glad you are because this journey would have been very tedious without your company.'

'What are you going to do when we get there?'

'I'm going to storm the Bastille.'

Mark looked worried. 'I'm no fighter you know.'

'Don't you worry.' James dropped his voice. 'Got exactly the right training for it. Did a lot of this in the SAS.' He laughed at Mark's expression. 'Anyway shouldn't be too long before you see me in action. Looks like we're landing.'

James had hired a car and they were sitting in it just down the street from the Palazzo Vasari. It had taken quite a bit of time to organize this trip so consequently they didn't get to Rome till 7 August. They'd been watching the house for a week and it was now 14 August. There hadn't been any sign of Carlo, or anyone else at the villa. Unfortunately they had been unable to spend twenty-four hours a day watching because they'd had to have toilet breaks and, of course, they'd had to go back to their hotel at night. And it was now over two months since James had seen Sarah.

'You know we could easily have missed something taking breaks. We should have organized ourselves properly, worked out a rota for sleeping etc,' said James.

'Yeah, but then we'd have needed two cars and I wouldn't have been any good at driving in Rome. I'm not used to driving in a foreign city, like you, mate. Sorry! Maybe you should have brought someone else.'

'No! Don't be daft. I'm glad I brought you. You've been a right good laugh.'

'Oh aye! Me and my cricket jokes.'

'Believe it or not, it's those jokes that have kept me sane.

Here, have some coffee and another sandwich. Shall we stay a bit longer tonight?'

'I reckon we should go and have a proper meal because I'm fed up with eating this stale cardboard. We can be back here by seven o'clock. Maybe Carlo returns at night. We've never stayed longer than seven.'

'Good idea.'

They were back at eight o'clock.

'Took a bit longer than we thought,' said Mark.

'Don't settle down. I can see some lights. Bingo! We've struck lucky.'

But it was ten o'clock before it was dark enough to risk breaking in. 'Now listen, Mark. You stay well behind me. If it all kicks off and someone threatens you with a gun, hold up your bandaged thumb and shout Manchester United.'

'What the hell for?'

'Because there are United fans all over the world and it always stops them dead in their tracks. And with a bit of luck they might think you're an injured United player.'

Mark didn't know much about football; he'd been too busy concentrating on his cricket over the years. 'Do you happen to know if United has ever beaten Roma?'

'No idea! I don't follow football. Rugby's always been my game. Anyway, don't worry about it. The one thing I do know, because I've seen it on the telly, is David Beckham is on loan to AC Milan at present so that should help things along.'

'Not in Rome it won't, you idiot.'

'Oh aye! Well, don't worry about it. I won't need any help and even if I did I wouldn't want you to get involved. Just follow my orders and keep yourself safe.'

Mark was astounded at the ease with which James got through the cast-iron gates. 'I didn't know you'd brought those.'

'Always come prepared,' said James stowing the special cutters back in his pocket. He had just snipped through the metal strut holding the hinges as easily as if it was made of plastic. 'Got to find an open window now.'

'Surely no one will have left a window open?'

'There's always a window open because there's always someone stupid enough to leave one open, even if it's only a lavatory window. Actually, more often than not, someone who's been having a crafty fag will leave a window open.' James was right. There was a small window open at the back of the villa. James bounded on to the windowsill. 'Wait here. I'll unlock the back door.' He disappeared from view. A few moments later a door opened to the left of Mark and they were both inside the building.

The next five minutes were the scariest of Mark's life. James raced down the corridors with his friend following. Every time a man appeared James knocked him to the ground. None of them stood a chance. Soon there were bodies everywhere. Unfortunately there was a bit too much noise and suddenly a door opened and Carlo stood there with a gun in his hand. He was flanked by two bodyguards, both pointing guns at James.

James skidded to a halt. 'What the hell have you done with Sarah?' he shouted.

'And what have you done to my men, James? And what are you doing here?'

'I'm here to put you straight, Carlo. Sarah's got hold of the wrong end of the stick.' He could see that Carlo didn't understand him. 'Sarah's wrong,' he yelled.

Mark was standing with both hands in the air. Suddenly he came to life, remembered what James had said and shouted, 'Manchester United,' as loud as he possibly could.

Carlo nearly dropped his gun and James burst out laughing.

Then Carlo started laughing. 'You two had better come inside.' Then he spoke in Italian to the two men and they went off down the corridor, leering at James and Mark who both scowled back. Carlo walked to the side of the corridor and stared at all the bodies. Then he turned and walked back into his office.

James and Mark followed him.

'Please sit down.' Carlo replaced the gun in his shoulder holster. 'Before you tell me what this is all about I would like to know how you got past my men. They are all highly trained bodyguards and yet I see them laid out on the floor. Have you used some sort of stun gun or gas maybe?'

'Nope! Just fists and feet.'

'I can hardly believe that.'

'My army training might have something to do with it. If I tell you, Carlo, it doesn't go any further: I was in the SAS.'

'That's a surprise. I take it Marilyn doesn't know.'

'No, she doesn't.'

'So why are you here? You must know Sarah doesn't want to see you ever again. What you did to us all was dishonourable.'

'It isn't true. I'm here to tell you exactly what happened and then you will have to judge whether I did right or wrong.'

Going through the same tale for the fourth time was very tedious. He'd told his mother, Jane, Mark and now Carlo knew.

'What a tale. I do believe you although I find it rather, how do you say? Far away from the truth.'

'I think you mean far-fetched.'

'*Sì*! What a dilemma for you. I think it is going to be difficult to convince the women. And I am afraid I have some bad news. Sarah had an accident just after a taxi driver brought her from the airport. A thief on a motor bike attacked her. You know the sort. They snatch a bag and drive away.'

'Oh! No! No! I knew something was wrong.' James was beside himself with fear. His hands were trembling.

'Do not worry, my friend. She was taken to hospital and she recovered enough to ask for Marilyn. We brought her here. My doctor has been seeing her. She had concussion. But she is recovered. She very much likes it here with Marilyn and she might even stay and start a new life here in Italy.'

'That's bloody ridiculous. She has a life and a business in England. I must see her at once.'

'I am sorry, you cannot at this minute. She isn't actually here. She is now at our country villa in the hills. And do not think of trying to find it because you won't.'

'You can't stop me from seeing her, Carlo.'

'And I will not. In fact, I will take you to her, but unfortunately I have some business to attend to before I go home. So you will have to stay here for a few days. You will be well looked after. And if you want to go sightseeing one of my men will drive you anywhere you want to go. They all speak good English, by the way.'

James was furious that he couldn't get to see Sarah straight away. Carlo's business, whatever it was, took much longer than he'd anticipated. He'd told James it would take ten days but it took three weeks and James was nearly out of his mind with worry. He had asked Carlo not to tell the women that he was coming to see Sarah because he was afraid that she might run away. Carlo agreed with him and promised to say nothing.

CHAPTER TWELVE

Meanwhile Sarah was having a wonderful time in Sicily, totally oblivious that the hours spent with Salvatore were coming to an end. Today they were down in the town of Cefalu. Salvatore had taken her to see the fishing boats lying on one of the sandy beaches. She was entranced by them. They were painted in the most vibrant colours. Starting at the gunnel, the boats had horizontal stripes of emerald green, cream, deep apricot, white and terracotta.

'What are those lanterns for?'

'The men take the boats out at night. They gather round in a circle and look for the fish in the water. Is very pretty. Maybe I take you out at midnight. *Sí?*'

Sarah stared into his eyes trying to work out if he meant it. The thought of sailing out into the moonlight with him was very enticing.

'Of course, unfortunately we wouldn't be alone.' He grinned shamelessly.

Sarah's thoughts returned to the scene around her. The bright Sicilian sun blazed down from a cornflower-blue sky. The sand looked like dark melted fudge. It was just like the picture a child, with a vivid imagination, would paint.

Salvatore was watching her. 'This is a most beautiful place. *Sì?*'

'Oh yes. I think it is absolutely gorgeous.'

'So maybe you might like to stay here forever, Sarah?'

Sarah dragged her gaze from the scene and stared at Savatore. What did he mean? Stay here forever? Was he asking her to marry him? She turned away from him and let her eyes wander across the waves. It was too soon for her to consider marriage. She decided to ignore him. She turned back to him and asked, 'Do you think we could find some shade? It's very hot today.'

He didn't flinch at the change of subject. He just continued to watch her for a few minutes. Then he held out his hand. 'We'll go and have a cool glass of lemon. No wine for you till this evening.'

Jolly good thing, thought Sarah. She very much wanted to keep her brain in gear. Salvatore had waited over two months before making another move, and she had to admire him for his restraint. For a brief moment she wondered what it would be like to be married to a Sicilian. Marilyn seemed happy with her life. And Salvatore was kind and sensitive as well as strong and she. . . . Her train of thought was interrupted.

'Sarah! Sarah! Come back to me. I thought you wanted to get out of the sun.'

'Oh! Sorry! I was miles away.' Then she remembered what she had been thinking. She loved him. Her face felt hot and she knew she was blushing.

'I think you have already got too much sun. Come on.' He dragged her up the beach and a few minutes later they were in a café sipping cold drinks.

After they had finished their drinks Salvatore was ready to be off again. 'We still have a few hours to kill so I now take you to see an island where we imprison our women.'

She assumed he was joking.

'So this is the village of Isola delle Femmine and there is the island.'

Sarah surveyed the small cone-shaped island about a hundred yards from the shore. There was a ruined tower on the highest point but that was all.

'Men of the village used to put their wives out there if they disobeyed them.'

'You're kidding me.'

'Not understand that word, Sarah.'

'It means you are teasing me.'

'Ah! *Sí*! No. Not teasing. Is true. So if you refuse to marry me, I will tie you up, put you in a boat and row you out to that island. Leave you there till you say yes.' He smiled at her. 'Just teasing this time, Sarah. Now we go and see more of Sicily.'

They got back in the car.

Sarah was glad to be back in her bedroom. She was removing her shorts and blouse ready for a shower. She had a lot to think about. It had been a bombshell to realize she was falling in love with Salvatore and she knew that the next time he kissed her she would not be able to refuse him anything. But it was one thing to surrender to his passionate lovemaking and quite another to marry him. A few months ago she'd been making plans to marry James. She wondered where he was and what he was doing. Maybe he was back in America; in Washington with Sandra. How could she have fallen in love with Salvatore so soon after James? Was she really so shallow that she could jump out of one bed into another without giving it a thought? She slipped into a pair of cream slacks and a moss-green silk blouse and went along to the dining-room. But dinner wasn't ready and the only person in the room was Salvatore. There was a question in his eyes. He took hold of her hand and led her out into the gardens.

The sun was setting. Orange streaks trailed across the midnight-blue sky and the horizon was dappled with opalescent clouds edged with bronze. In the distance the mountains formed a dark mahogany circle, shielding the villa from the eyes of the world. They walked in silence until they were hidden from the windows of the villa. It seemed they both knew that they didn't want anyone to see them. At last they came to the bottom of the garden and Salvatore pulled her into his arms.

Sarah was floating on air. He was kissing her neck and his kisses sent her pulse racing. He ran his hands down her body. Her silk blouse felt paper-thin and his light caresses set her on fire. She followed him as he sank down on to the grass. The grass was warm from the day's sunshine and it had that wonderful salty seaside smell.

Salvatore pushed her back until she was lying in his arms and kissed her again.

'You know what I want, Sarah.' He pulled back slightly and looked into her eyes. 'You are ready I think. I also think we should go to my room where no one can watch us.'

'No, wait.'

'For what, Sarah?'

'For this.' She put a hand around his neck, pulled him back down and kissed him tenderly. She put everything she was feeling into the kiss. She pressed her body closer and she knew he felt her desire. She was already physically aroused and she didn't want to wait any longer. She wanted to feel his bare skin next to hers. She started to unbutton his shirt.

'No, Sarah. Not here where we can be seen.'

'Oh, James, don't be so prudish,' she giggled. She gasped in alarm as he pushed her violently away from him. 'What's the matter? What's wrong?'

'His name. You said *his* name.' Then Salvatore burst into a torrent of Italian.

Sarah stared in horror at him. 'I'm sorry,' she stuttered. 'It was. . . . It was just a slip of the tongue. I love you, Salvatore. Please believe me.' She burst into tears.

He started speaking in English again. 'Why do you still think of him then? He uses you and still you call his name. He defiles you. He is married already. He was married when he married our Marilyn. He was a. . . .' He struggled to find the word but before he could remember, a waterfall cascaded over them.

Sarah screamed. She was soaking. What the hell was happening? Then she realized the lawn sprinklers had just come on. Before she could stand up and run inside, the whole garden was flooded with light as several black limousines swept up the drive.

Unknown to Sarah the first and third ones carried Carlo's bodyguards but the second one carried Carlo, Mark and James. The powerful headlights had illuminated the two figures lying on the grass. And James had seen everything. He leapt out of the car while it was still moving, ran across the grass, bent down and punched Salvatore in the face. Salvatore collapsed like a rag doll. Sarah started screaming, but before James could get stuck in any further, six bodyguards had pounced on him.

CHAPTER THIRTEEN

They were all in the garden. Carlo, Salvatore, Marilyn, Sarah, James, Mark and last, but by no means least, six bodyguards who had travelled from Rome with Carlo. There were also a few more staff, who had rushed out of the villa when they heard the commotion. Some of the bodyguards were standing over James. One was guarding Mark. And Carlo had Salvatore in a grip of steel. The two Sicilians were arguing furiously in their own language and Salvatore was looking decidedly sulky.

'What are they saying?' Sarah asked Marilyn.

'It's not always possible for me to translate. Sicilian isn't like Italian, but I think Carlo is trying to persuade Salvatore not to kill James. But he's not going to stop me killing him.'

'And me.' Sarah suddenly remembered the children. 'Where are the children?'

'Maria is giving them some dinner. I've given her strict instructions to keep them inside and put them to bed. And now I'm going to have a little word with James.' She marched over with Sarah in tow. 'So what the hell do you mean by marrying me when you were already married?' Marilyn snarled, and then she slapped him across his face so hard that a bright red impression of her fingers flared on his cheek. 'I've been longing to do that for two months.'

'No!' shouted Carlo as he came running over. 'You make mistake.' He grabbed her arm and started talking in Italian, but she was having none of it.

'Speak English to me, Carlo. I am not following you.' Her eyes glittered with rage. 'Why have you brought him here?'

Salvatore immediately took advantage of the fact that Carlo now had his hands full with Marilyn. He walked over and grabbed Sarah's arm. 'Come with me.' He dragged her into the villa. 'Did you know he was coming here?'

'No, I didn't. How can you think that?'

'I am sorry, Sarah, but I love you so much and now James has come to take you away from me.'

'I'm not going with him. I love you, Salvatore, not James. I'm going to my bedroom. I'll pack my clothes and you can take me away. Will you do that for me?'

'Yes, I will. We go tonight while they are not looking at us. Quickly.' He marched off towards Sarah's rooms and she followed.

Outside, all hell was breaking loose as James tried to follow Sarah and it took six men to hang on to him. 'Get off me,' he shouted. 'Carlo, tell them to let me go. That bastard has just dragged Sarah away.'

'That bastard, as you dare to put it,' snapped Marilyn, 'is my brother-in-law. He is a kind and honourable man, which is more than I can say for you. And, what's more he's in love with Sarah and she'll be much better off with him than you.'

'Marilyn!' Carlo grabbed her. 'James is not married to that American and he never has been.'

'I don't believe you.'

'I can prove it,' James yelled.

'James, will you stop shouting. I don't want my children to

hear all this.'

'I'm sorry, Carlo. I won't shout again but will you please, please go and see what that man is up to with Sarah?'

'My brother is her friend. He will just be comforting her. However, I will go and find them. While I do, you must tell Marilyn everything that you tell me in Rome and then we will all meet up in the sitting-room and have . . . how you say? We will have a confirmation. *Sí?*'

'You mean a conference,' said James, wearily.

'Who's that?' Marilyn pointed at Mark.

'I'm his bodyguard,' Mark shouted.

James laughed, in spite of the seriousness of the situation. 'Carlo, call off your bulldogs, will you? I promise I'll behave myself, even if your wife slaps me again.'

Carlo shouted some instructions to his men and they faded into the shadows.

'Please, Marilyn, can we go inside and I'll tell you everything?'

But Marilyn turned her back on James and marched off.

James, Mark and Carlo followed her.

Once inside, Carlo asked Marilyn if she would look after the two men while he went to fetch Sarah and Salvatore. 'Please, Marilyn. These are our guests. Look after them properly. I promise, James has done no wrong.'

As soon as Carlo left the room, Marilyn rounded on James. She was spitting mad. 'You may have pulled the wool over my husband's eyes but you can't fool me as easily, or Sarah either, and don't you dare try to bully her into going back with you.'

James knew Marilyn had a temper and he thought it best to ignore her.

Carlo walked into Sarah's bedroom. Sarah was emptying the

drawers as fast as possible and throwing her clothes to Salvatore who was dumping them in her trolley bag.

Carlo shouted, grabbed Salvatore and shoved him out of the bedroom.

'What did you say to him?'

'I told him to get out while I speak to you.' Carlo shut the bedroom door. 'Don't worry, he's waiting just outside the door, but you aren't going anywhere.'

'Yes I am. I'm going away with Salvatore. Far away where James can never find me ever again.' She stared defiantly at Carlo.

'When you've heard what James has to say, then you can go, but you might change your mind when you've heard everything.'

'I don't think so.'

'For Marilyn's sake, please come and speak to James.'

Sarah hesitated. She suddenly felt ashamed for bringing so much trouble into Carlo's house. He had been very kind to her and so had Marilyn. They didn't deserve all this. 'I'm sorry,' she whispered. 'I'll come down and listen to what he has to say. I'm sorry I've brought all this trouble into your home.'

'Do not be upset. It's not your fault. In any case, it has been wonderful for Marilyn. She has loved having you. We all have. It has been a pleasure.'

Sarah and Salvatore followed Carlo into the sitting-room. Sarah made sure she was sitting as far away from James as possible.

He started telling his side of things but his voice faded away as he saw the hard expression on Sarah's face. He knew she would never believe him. The story sounded like a fairy-tale, even to his ears. He stopped speaking and sighed. He stood up.

'Where are you going James?'

'I'm going home, Carlo. Home to Scotland.'

'No. You've come too far. You told me how you could prove it and we'll do that. We will all fly to Washington. My family has some unfinished business in New York that I myself must sort. We can join everything together. I know when you show these two wild tigers what you've told me, they will be convinced.'

James was totally overwhelmed by Carlo's offer but he knew he couldn't accept it. 'I can't let you do that.'

'It will be worth it, James, just to get things back to normal.'

CHAPTER FOURTEEN

'I don't believe we let ourselves be persuaded to come on this trip,' said Sarah to Marilyn. She was again sitting as far away as possible from James. The two women were at the back. James and Carlo were at the front and Salvatore was sitting with Mark in the centre of the plane. There were two bodyguards separating James from Salvatore.

'Me, too. But here we are on our way to America. It's a good job all our passports were in order.'

'I used to go to America when Tony was alive, trying to find new outlets for our jewellery. So I always kept my passport up to date. It's lucky that Carlo was able to get me a duplicate passport. And James goes to New York all the time.'

James thought he'd have a bit of fun.

'Bodyguards are a bit thin on the ground.'

'I didn't think you needed any, James,' Carlo was quick to reply. He grinned at James. The two men were once again on good terms. Carlo had decided to trust him. 'I was very impressed by the way you disposed of the last lot. Your army training must come in very useful from time to time. However, if you feel you are in any danger, please be certain you are not. I have some more family meeting us at Dulles Airport and they will take care of us,' he teased him.

'Blimey, Carlo. You do seem to have rather a large family.'

'This is the American branch of the Vasari family. By the way, I'm sorry that Sarah wouldn't sit with you. I think they want to talk about you.'

'I know. I'm glad I can't hear what they're saying.'

'Ah, *sí*! Yes, I do believe they will not be saying nice things about you but it will all be sorted out in Washington.'

'This girl? Sandra? Do you think James has been in touch with her?'

'I certainly do. I reckon he will have primed her with a good story.'

'You don't trust James any more, do you?'

'No, I don't. This is the second time. . . .' Sarah stopped speaking. She had no wish to talk about Tony and so she changed the subject. 'Can I ask you a personal question?'

'Of course you can. I regard you as a very special friend. And friends can ask one another everything.'

'How come Carlo can afford a private jet? This is so gorgeous.' She stared round at the plush cream leather armchairs and all the beautiful walnut fittings.

'It doesn't just belong to Carlo. It belongs to the family. It's what you call a business perk.'

Sarah thought Marilyn sounded a bit vague and she was beginning to have her own suspicions about why the Vasari family seemed to be one of the richest families in Italy. 'What does Salvatore do for a living?'

'You mean he hasn't told you?'

'No. We never got round to talking business.' Sarah blushed.

'I'll bet you didn't. It's not my job to tell you. I'm sure he'll tell you when he's ready and it will probably be a nice surprise.'

Sarah had a feeling it would be more of a nasty shock than a nice surprise but she didn't say so to her new friend. She felt sorry for Marilyn. She was a bit naïve and she didn't seem to care that she might have married into... Stop it, she told herself. It wasn't right to think horrid thoughts about a family who had made her so welcome.

'Why don't you put your seat back and have a nap? You look tired. It's going to take a long time to get to Washington.' Marilyn beckoned to one of the bodyguards who were also acting as stewards. 'Can you please help Signora Livingstone with her seat? She wishes to have a sleep.'

But Sarah couldn't sleep. It had been a real shock seeing James arrive. She'd had no idea that he would be so persistent. And she'd really thought that he would never find her in Sicily. It wasn't fair of him to turn up like this. She'd been ready to give up her life in England to marry Salvatore and James had spoiled it all.

Eventually the novelty of travelling in style on a private jet started to wear off and the flight became tedious. They refuelled in Newfoundland. Sarah eventually slept and between naps meals were served.

At last they landed at Dulles Airport and sure enough there was a convoy of black sedans waiting for them. There was also another car waiting. It looked like there was some high-profile official inside because there was a uniformed chauffeur standing by the back door. As soon as he saw James he opened the door and a lady got out and ran towards them. James embraced her.

'Well, that's not Sandra,' whispered Sarah. 'She's far too old.' She looked as old as Elizabeth.

Then a very distinguished man joined her and gave James a bear hug. Then they turned away, went back to their car and got in.

'Two friends of mine,' said James. 'They are going to show your drivers where to go, Carlo. We just have to follow them. By the way, we have special permission to drive round the cemetery. It's not normally allowed, except for funerals. Ordinary visitors are expected to take what is called the Tourmobile Shuttle. We've also got an official escort. My friend is a senator and he has arranged everything.'

'What cemetery?' Sarah whispered to Marilyn and was met by a blank look.

Carlo looked uncomfortable, but then he seemed to recover his composure. 'Very well, James. I suggest you and I go with Marilyn and Sarah in one car and Salvatore goes with Mark in another.' There were four sedans.

At last they drove through the gates of Arlington Cemetery. A soldier in uniform saluted them as the convoy fell in behind an army jeep. Looking for all the world like a funeral procession, they wove their way along the paths between the beautiful lawns and graceful trees. When they finally stopped, the army jeep drove away.

The senator and his wife got out and walked on to the grass and down between two lines of identical memorial stones. James and his party followed. Sarah noticed James seemed to be walking quite slowly. He obviously wanted to give the two people in front time to reach a particular gravestone and when they did stop, James held back for a few minutes. Sarah watched the two people. They seemed to be praying.

Sarah gazed around. There were thousands and thousands of headstones, all the same height, fashioned from the same pure white marble; all with similar engravings. They stretched into the distance; line upon line, fanning out into a geometric pattern that confused her brain. The occupants of the graves couldn't have had a more beautiful setting in which to sleep till the end of time. It was nearly September and some of the trees were already turning different shades of golden-bronze. Soon it would be winter and the snow would cover the ground and the white marble stones would probably be almost invisible against the snow. The senator and his wife bowed their heads slightly.

James moved towards them. Everyone followed. They all looked at the headstone. Sarah was bewildered. There was a cross engraved in the marble. Beneath that were the words; James Charles Ross. Medal of Honor. Major. How could this be? She also saw the name of the unit and then some dates *January 14 1960* followed by *January 30 1990*. Suddenly it dawned on her; this was another James Ross and he was an American. James bent his head but not before Sarah had seen the tears running down his cheeks.

The senator and his wife had taken up position on either side of James. She put an arm round his shoulders, murmuring something that Sarah couldn't hear.

The senator looked at everyone. 'I would like us to drive to the Memorial Amphitheater where, seeing as the weather is so clement, we can sit in the open air. I know James has a story to tell you about our son and it is long and complicated.'

They returned to the cars, but this time James got in the senator's car.

The Memorial Amphitheater was one of the most beautiful buildings Sarah had ever seen. It looked like a Grecian temple with its graceful Doric columns, carved in pure white marble. There were hundreds of semi-circular benches inside. James went down the steps and sat down. Everyone gathered round. Some sat on the bench behind; some on the one in front. They could all hear him when he began to speak.

'I first met Jamie Ross at a special jungle warfare training school run by the British Military Garrison in Brunei. He was a member of Delta Force. I was in the SAS. We were both taking part in a cross-training operation. It's not unusual. The really unusual thing was we both had the same name. Luckily I was always known as James whereas my American counterpart had always been called Jamie. I won't go into too much detail but we were on a training exercise when I rather stupidly fell down a gully. It was a long way down and I lost my backpack and any means of communication. I was down there three days. It was pretty ghastly. The nights were particularly bad and I didn't think anyone would find me. Thought the end had come. Jamie led a rescue attempt and he was the one who climbed down to search for me. He risked his own life to save me. It had taken him three days to find me, but he simply wouldn't give up. Every serviceman will tell you about the strong friendships you develop in the army, particularly in the SAS and Delta Force, but there are no stronger ties than the ones that bind you to a man who has saved your life. Jamie and I became very close.' He stopped speaking.

Everyone could see that telling this story was putting him under a great strain but nobody spoke. Nobody interrupted him because they were all enthralled. Listening to an SAS officer talk about his time in the service wasn't an everyday occurrence.

'I was lucky. I only sprained my ankle but I was very dehydrated. I was in the army hospital for a few weeks and while I was there I developed, what one could only call, a crush on one of the nurses. I call it that because she totally ignored me. As a matter of fact, every bloody fellow who spent time in there fell madly in love with her. She was like an angel from heaven. She was called Sandra Mason. It was while Jamie was visiting me that he also fell under Sandra's spell.' James gazed into space.

Sarah knew he was remembering his wife and it was

obvious he still loved her. She couldn't think why he had dumped her in America.

He started to speak again. 'Then there came a day when we were sent on a mission to rescue some scientists in Sarawak. After two weeks of not hearing from them, the firm that had organized the expedition contacted the authorities. It took us three weeks to find them. Out of the twelve scientists only seven had survived and they were barely alive. We couldn't get a helicopter in so we had to carry them forty miles. Anyway we got the living out and delivered them safely to a hospital and then we went back for the rest. We were about halfway back when Jamie slipped down a ravine and broke his neck. He died instantly.' James started to cry.

Senator and Mrs Ross, who were sitting on either side of him, moved closer and spoke in low voices.

Senator Ross took up the story. 'My son was dead and the men already had a hell of a job on their hands, trying to carry out the others. They decided to leave two of the scientists with my son, to lighten the load. James climbed down into the ravine and stayed by my son's body until another retrieval mission could be organized. He was there a week. But this time he had enough food and water and he had protection against the weather and any wild creatures. But it must have been a hideous nightmare. We can never thank him enough for bringing Jamie's body back so we could give him a proper burial. We think of James as Jamie's brother. He is like a second son to us.'

Everyone listening looked shattered. Marilyn was crying into a handkerchief. Sarah felt sick as she thought of that young soldier with his whole life still in front of him. And she looked in sorrow at his parents, who had spent the last eighteen years without him.

James had recovered his composure and was able to carry

on with the sad tale. 'A few days after we all got back to Brunei, I had a visit from Sandra. She was pregnant. She had been seeing Jamie in secret and they were planning to marry.'

Senator Ross suddenly looked up. 'What did you say, James? Planning?'

'I am deeply sorry, sir. All these years I have deceived you, but it was in a good cause and I pray with all my heart that you will eventually forgive me. It was a shock to find out she was pregnant and I was at panic stations. I couldn't think what to do. After a few days I devised what I thought was a brilliant plan. I took Sandra over the border, into Malaysia and, pretending to be Jamie, I married her myself. I had papers which showed the same name. The crazy part is we both had the same middle names as well. This must be due to your Scottish ancestors,' James tried to raise a smile from the senator but it didn't work. He was staring at James horrified. His wife had only just cottoned on to what James was saying and she too looked appalled. 'I had to do it. I did it for Jamie and it's what he would have wanted. Sandra needed a father for her baby and I presumed you would want to look after Jamie's son. He is, after all, your grandson and living proof of Jamie's love for Sandra.'

'You brought her into America under false pretences. My God. Do you realize what a mess we're in?' Senator Ross bellowed.

His wife started to cry. 'Please don't shout, dear. If it hadn't been for James we would never have seen our grandson. And Jamie's body would have been left out there.'

Sarah was also aghast. 'But why didn't you get a divorce, James?'

'Quite simply, because I didn't need one.'

Marilyn gasped in horror at his cavalier attitude.

And Sarah stared at him in total confusion.

'Will you please listen? I didn't need a divorce because the marriage wasn't legal. The bloke wasn't licensed to perform marriages. You see, we had decided to do it in secret so we could get the certificate backdated. And I had been charged a lot of money for that privilege. Bloke obviously saw a chance to make a packet. It was only when I got a solicitor on to the job that he found out it wasn't legal. I should have realized at the time there was something fishy about it because he gave us two copies of the certificate. Said it was so we could have one each. I mean! Why would a married couple need two marriage certificates?'

They had all drifted out of the circle of marble leaving James talking to Senator Ross and his wife. Marilyn was standing with Sarah and Mark. A few yards away stood Carlo and Salvatore, talking earnestly.

Mark was the first to break the silence. 'Well, that's a turn-up for the books.'

Sarah looked distinctly uncomfortable. 'I should have trusted him,' she muttered. 'And I don't know how I'm going to apologize to him, or to you, Marilyn.'

'Don't be silly. You weren't to know. Anyway if you hadn't jumped to the wrong conclusion you wouldn't have come to find us and you wouldn't have fallen in love with Salvatore.'

Mark looked at Marilyn in dismay. 'What?'

Marilyn realized her mistake. 'Just forget you heard that.'

But Mark had no intention of forgetting it. He grabbed Sarah's arm and dragged her away from Marilyn. 'What the hell is she talking about? Do you know, James has spent months and months looking for you? He even hired a private detective and d'you know what he found out? That bloody Vasari family is part of the Mafia. How the hell can you be in love with someone like that?'

Sarah pushed him away. She didn't want to listen. Things

were bad enough without Mark having a go at her. 'I'm not in love with him, so you'd better not say anything to James.' She saw James coming up the steps of the amphitheater and she ran towards him. 'I'm truly sorry, James.' There were tears in her eyes.

James looked drained of emotion, as well he might. 'It doesn't matter anymore. Nothing matters to me anymore. Listen, we've been invited to stay with the senator and his wife for a few days. They want you to meet Sandra and Jamie.'

'What's going to happen to them?' Sarah whispered. 'I couldn't bear it if Sandra lost her home and was deported. It's all my fault. She's English, isn't she?'

James nodded. 'Yes, but don't worry. Senator Ross wants nothing more said about this. There is no doubt in their minds that Sandra's son is their grandchild. We are just going to pretend that the certificate is valid. No one is ever going to question it.'

Carlo had just walked over. 'So! You make big mess, James. We are all very sorry about what happened to your friend. Is his family all right with it now?'

'Yes. They want us to stay for a few days so Sarah can meet Sandra and Jamie.'

'That is good. I have business in New York. We will fly there. It only take me a few days then I can return and you might as well fly home with me. *Sí*? You all have your bags. We will fly to Roma first and then you and your friends can continue to England.'

'That is extremely kind of you.'

'Is no bother, James. We are all good friends. We see you in a few days. I phone you when we are ready to come back.'

He walked away and suddenly Sarah was aware that Senator and Mrs Ross had joined them.

'James has asked you to come and stay with us, has he?'
'Yes. It's very kind of you.'
'Actually it's entirely selfish of us. We love James so much and it's just an excuse to keep him close for a bit longer.' She tucked her arm in Sarah's.

As they made their way to the car Sarah saw that Carlo and his extended family had already left.

They drove back through Arlington Cemetery and stopped at another grave. 'We thought you should see President Kennedy's grave before you leave America.'

They gazed at the stone laid low on the ground. It was a five-foot piece of rough granite that looked rather like a stone-age wheel. There in the centre was the brave little flame that was never allowed to go out: the Eternal Flame. It was a very emotional moment. The senator was telling them that the irregular paving stones around the grave area were made of Cape Cod granite, but Sarah was only half listening. She felt her heart was breaking because she knew it was the end of the road for her and Salvatore.

The senator and his wife lived across the River Potomac from Arlington Cemetery in Georgetown. Sarah was hardly aware of the journey to their home. All she could think about was the fact that she loved Salvatore with all her heart and always would. She knew that Jane had been right when she accused her of falling for James again because it was an easy option. How on earth could she tell him? She did love James, but it was the love one would feel for a dear friend. That special spark wasn't there. Maybe falling in love with Salvatore had made her realize that while one emotion was passion the other was merely affection. She suddenly thought to herself how isolated she was. Once again she was alone in a strange city with no one to help her. And this time she couldn't turn to James.

A servant answered the door of the gracious Georgetown mansion. He took their coats. The senator led them into a sitting-room. No sooner had they sat down than a young cadet burst into the room. Even if Sarah still held any doubts about whether James was telling the truth, it was obvious that this boy could never be his son. Everywhere you looked, there were photos of the senator's son Jamie and this boy was the absolute spit of his American father. Then a young woman with long blonde hair walked into the room.

The room was suddenly flooded with light from the love shining out of Sandra's eyes, but James was too stupid to notice. Just how thick can men get, Sarah wondered to herself? Anybody looking at Sandra could clearly see that even if she had been in love with the American soldier all those years ago, she was now deeply in love with the man who had brought her to Washington. What a mess!

It was late evening when Sarah found herself alone with James. This was going to be very tricky but it had to be done.

'What do you think of Sandra and Jamie?'

'I think Sandra is exquisite and Jamie is just like his father. It must be very painful for the senator and his wife.'

'Actually I don't think it is. It seems to have helped them come to terms with their loss. You know he is going to follow in his father's footsteps? There have been generations of Ross army men and all of them made it to general. All of them except one,' he added sadly.

'No, two,' Sarah corrected. 'You.'

'Oh yes, me.' James smiled. 'Well, Sarah, here we are, back where we started.'

'Not quite, James. Now there are three of us.'

His face lit up. 'You can't mean—'

Sarah realized what he was thinking. 'Good God, no. I certainly do not mean I'm pregnant, you dope. I meant

Sandra. She's the third person.'

James wrinkled his forehead. 'I don't understand.'

'Sandra is in love with you.'

'Don't be ridiculous. You're mistaking love for gratitude. She's always treated me as if I am her guardian angel. I usually take it with a pinch of salt.'

'You need a bucket of salt then, because that gratitude, over the years, has turned to love. If you don't believe me, ask Mrs Ross.'

'Why are you doing this, Sarah?' James growled. 'Is this just so you can get rid of me and fly away with that cocky little Sicilian?'

'How dare you!' Sarah was furious. 'I am never going to see him again.'

'How can you say that? We'll be flying home with them. You'll see him then.'

Sarah thought her heart was breaking as she answered him. 'I may be in the same plane with him, but believe me when I tell you, there is nothing between us and never will be, ever. So you can stop inventing excuses and go and ask Sandra, straight out if I'm right. Are you afraid? You fell in love with her once. What's happened to change things between you?'

'I suppose I wanted her to stay true to Jamie,' he muttered, miserably. 'I kept my feelings in check because I, too, wanted to honour his memory. I thought I had killed off any real feelings for her, but I always looked after her.' He stared defiantly at Sarah.

'Oh God, James. You can't ask her to tie herself to a ghost for the rest of her life and you must know in your heart that it isn't what Jamie would have wanted. In fact, I'm sure he's looking down on you right now and begging you to marry her. Wasn't she your first love. Well, just like in the song, she can be your last love. You must go to her and tell her you love her. And you should do it now. Remember, James, sometimes life is very short. You only get one chance at happiness. Jamie didn't even get one.' And with that parting shot she left him and went up to the bedroom that had been allocated to her.

The following morning she looked on to a garden that wouldn't have been out of place in the grounds of Hampton Court. And there under the trees was James with his arms wrapped around Sandra. Her arms were around his neck and they were kissing one another. Evidently James had at last realized what must have been under his nose for years. Sarah hurriedly showered and dressed, eager to get downstairs and congratulate them. She felt no jealousy at all. She was happy they had found each other at last.

While they were waiting for Carlo to come back to Washington, Mrs Ross took Sarah on a number of sightseeing trips. 'Keeps us out of the young lovers' hair.'

'Don't you mind about Sandra being in love with James?'

'Not at all. My husband and I have seen it coming for years. We were quite upset that James seemed to be blind to it.'

Then came the phone call that Sarah had been dreading and a car took them back over the Potomac to Dulles International Airport.

'You're very quiet. Sarah. May I say something personal?'

'If you feel you must, James.'

'If there is any chance that you do love Salvatore, you must tell him. Otherwise, take it from me, you will, as you said, never see him again after today.'

Sarah ignored the advice. There was no way she was going to marry into a family with Mafia connections.

It was an excruciating meeting. Everyone was very polite as they boarded the Boeing. Maybe Carlo had told Salvatore to leave Sarah alone now they thought she was back with James. Sarah had no intention of enlightening them. It would be easier this way.

CHAPTER FIFTEEN

It was just after take-off that it happened.

'Hands in the air, now!' yelled the steward, brandishing a gun. At the same time two more armed men burst out of the lavatories.

Marilyn and Sarah screamed.

James knew he had to keep everyone calm. 'Shut up and don't move,' he shouted at the women.

Salvatore and Carlo were motionless with their hands in the air.

The men had American accents but were clearly Italian. This had to have something to do with Carlo's family business. Another man appeared from the cockpit. James assessed the chances of overpowering them. Four of them. Three of us. Oh no. Four if he counted Mark. Maybe it was possible. Suddenly one of the men poked him in the ribs with his gun.

'Stick your hands out.'

James did exactly what he was told.

'You!' The gunman pointed at Sarah. 'Come here.'

She looked at James and he nodded. She stood up and walked over.

'Tie his hands together with this.' The man produced some

rope from under the seat and shoved it into Sarah's trembling hands.

Mistake number one, thought James. It was always far more difficult to escape if your hands were tied behind your back. However, the rope under the seat told him they had been well prepared. As Sarah bent down, he whispered, 'Do what they tell you. No arguments. Stay detached. Tell the others what I've said.' He was hoping she would get the chance to do just that. And she did. Mistake number two, thought James. Sarah had been told to tie the others up and she now had the opportunity to pass on his message.

As Sarah bent over Marilyn, the look on her face told James she had heard his message but she still looked like she was going to faint. The three other men just looked blank. Good! The plane was ascending smoothly. Either it was Carlo's pilot, flying it with a gun to his head, or the kidnappers had their own experienced pilot. James tried to work out how many gunmen there were. Four here in the cabin and maybe two or three more in the cockpit.

Eventually the men sat down but they still had their guns trained on the hostages. James wondered if they knew what could happen if they fired a gun inside an aircraft. He now had the chance to look out of the window to his left. The sun was shining right into his eyes and he was facing the cockpit. He glanced at his watch. Half past ten. So that meant they were flying south. Miami maybe, or the Caribbean. Cuba? Haiti? Somewhere in South America? How much fuel was there? Would they have to refuel? Would there be a better chance on the ground? It was about 2,000 miles to Mexico and if that was the destination they wouldn't need to refuel which was a pity because if they did land anywhere, the ground staff might notice something was wrong.

They had been flying three hours when James realized they

were descending. Turning his head very, very slightly, he glanced out of the window. He caught a view of jungle-covered mountains and saw something he recognized from his days in the SAS. He often used to spend his spare time staring at types of terrain all round the world, just in case they ever ended up there. He could see the massive limestone humps that some people called the sugar-loaf mountains. They were covered with green vegetation and they rose straight up from the flat plains of Pinar del Rio. So they were flying over Cuba. Then he saw another stretch of water and then they were circling and landing. Landing on what? Landing on a very bumpy runway. The plane skewed to a halt.

The men jumped to their feet and started yelling. 'Stay where you are. No one move.' Two of the men grabbed Carlo and dragged him to the other end of the cabin. They started gabbling in Italian to him. Meanwhile the other two men went to each of the prisoners in turn and rifled through jackets and bags. Out came the mobile phones to be chucked into a plastic bag. Their passports and wallets were taken away from them. One of the men flicked through the passports. He swore suddenly and started talking in Italian again to his companion. James heard some words he recognized. Manchester. They were talking about Sarah. SAS. What? SAS? How the hell did they know that? That bit of information certainly wasn't on his passport.

While they were engrossed, looking at the passports, Carlo turned his head and looked straight at James. He mouthed one word. No! Then he turned his head away.

James had no idea what message he was trying to send. His best bet was that Carlo didn't want him to react in any way. James stared out of the window. Out of the corner of his eye he could see Salvatore fidgeting in his seat.

One of the men ran back to the prisoners. He was obviously rather wound up. He was shouting in Italian and waving his gun around. The others were shouting back and Carlo was struggling. Then the man pointed the gun at Sarah.

James had absolutely no idea how it happened but suddenly Salvatore was on his feet, throwing himself in front of the gunman. The gun went off with a deafening bang. Everyone screamed as James watched in horror. It was almost like a slow-motion film. Salvatore fell backwards on top of Sarah, crushing her. Blood blossomed from the wound. Bucketloads of it. And James knew instinctively that the bullet had found the sub-clavian artery, which was near the clavicle or collarbone. It was a large artery and it carried blood away from the heart.

As an SAS officer, James was trained to know a great deal about bullet wounds and how to treat them but even if his hands had been free, he couldn't have helped the Sicilian because if he wasn't already dead he soon would be. James felt helpless. His chin sank on to his chest. He thought about every operation he'd ever been on. He'd survived them all yet here he was, immobilized by what seemed like an incompetent bunch of New York gangsters who looked as though they were about to kill everyone on the plane.

The men who were holding Carlo dragged him to the cabin door. One of the men, obviously the leader of the pack, used his own gun to hit the killer across his face. He shouted something at him and then he opened the cabin door and looked out.

James heard the rumble of a heavy truck getting nearer. Eventually it sounded as though it was right outside. Two of the men left the cabin. Another ran back into the cockpit and several gunshots were heard. Then he came running back with another man, obviously their own pilot, thought James.

They grabbed Carlo and forced him out of the door.

Marilyn started screaming.

Carlo turned his head and shouted so loud, he drowned out Marilyn's screams, 'Shut your mouth, you stupid bitch!'

Marilyn was shocked into silence.

James had a good idea why Carlo had treated her like that. He had found a British passport under the restaurant table in Mallorca and he had looked inside it to find out whose it was. The name in it was Marilyn Ross. When he had given it back to her, he had asked why she was still calling herself Ross. She had told him that Carlo didn't want anyone to know she was his wife and that he had made her keep her old married name. She had also said she didn't know whether it was strictly legal to renew it like that but she had.

'In God's name, why doesn't Carlo want people to know you're married to him?'

'Because if we ever get kidnapped Carlo said I might get treated better if I had a British passport and no one knew I was a Vasari.'

James thought Carlo knew more about the gangster world than he let on.

He was brought back to the present by the sound of engines revving. The transport, whatever it was, seemed to be moving off. The engine noise receded into the distance until all he could hear was the squawking of some unfamiliar birds.

CHAPTER SIXTEEN

James was fairly sure that their kidnappers had gone. His heart was racing. Should he risk going to have a look? He got unsteadily to his feet, staggered to the door and looked out. The runway, such as it was, was totally deserted. There were some buildings in the distance but they, too, were deserted. There was no sign of any ground support staff. This place looked as though it hadn't been used for a good few years. He suddenly heard Marilyn shouting. He turned round.

'James!' Marilyn screamed. 'Help Salvatore. Please.'

James didn't like to say that there was no point in helping Salvatore but then he realized that Sarah was trapped underneath him. The Sicilian might have saved her from a bullet but it was likely that she was being crushed to death. He went over to Mark.

'They've gone. Those bastards made a big mistake when they tied our hands at the front instead of at the back. It means you can help me to get rid of this rope.'

Mark started to undo the knots, but even though his hands were tied in front of him, it was still a very slow process. 'You know that special cutting tool—'

James interrupted him. 'Forget it, mate. It's in my bloody bag in the bloody hold.' James was furious with himself.

'Well, you weren't to know this would happen.' Mark was still struggling.

James tried not to look impatient. Mark was doing his very best under the circumstances. But all the time he was waiting, he knew Sarah could be slipping away. There had been no sound from her. At last the ropes fell off. He set Mark free as quickly as possible. 'Untie Marilyn. I'll see to Sarah.' He darted to the back of the plane. As he started to lift Salvatore he got a hell of a shock. The Sicilian was still breathing. 'Mark!' he shouted. 'Get over here, quick. Salvatore's still alive.'

Between them they carefully lifted him and laid him on the carpet between the seats. Sarah was still breathing as well and was starting to moan.

'Look here,' said Mark. 'She must have hit her head.'

'We'll have to leave her and see to Salvatore first. I'll have to try and stop this damn bleeding. I was sure that bullet hit an artery, but I must be wrong because if it had he'd be dead by now.'

'Can you get the bullet out?'

'Not if it's gone too deep. Best leave it for a surgeon. Find the first-aid box.'

Mark returned with one. 'What's the point of leaving it to a surgeon? In case you hadn't noticed, we ain't near a hospital, we're in the middle of a bloody jungle.'

'Yes, and I can do a lot more damage if I go digging around in his shoulder. Could kill him. This way if we try and keep the bleeding to the minimum and stop any infection getting in the wound, he might survive.' He used the large scissors from the first-aid box to cut through Salvatore's coat and shirt leaving the whole of his chest bare. 'Wish we'd known about these scissors earlier.'

Marilyn looked like she was going to be sick when she saw the wound.

Mark used some words he never normally used in front of a woman.

James ignored both of them. He poured liquid antiseptic into the wound. 'Good job he's out of it because this would hurt like crazy. Can you find a blanket, Marilyn?'

She went off to get one, while James taped a large sterile pad over the wound and then she returned with a blanket and a pillow.

'Good thinking.' He placed the pillow carefully under the Sicilian's head and covered him with the blanket. 'Right. That's it. We'll have to move him somewhere more comfortable later, but now we'll have to see to Sarah.'

Marilyn had disappeared again but was soon back. 'Here. I got this from the galley.' She was carrying a bowl of iced water and some towels.

James lifted Sarah's head, dipped the towel in amongst the ice cubes and then applied it to her forehead. She started to come round. 'Ah good. You're back with us.'

'What happened?' she moaned.

'Your boyfriend saved your life.'

'Oh my God.' Sarah suddenly remembered. 'Where is he?' She clutched his arm. 'He's dead isn't he?'

'No, but he's very badly injured. We have got to get him to a hospital. If you can stand up, I want you to look after him. I need to talk to Mark and Marilyn.'

'What about Carlo?' Marilyn looked as though she was going to have a panic attack.

'Don't worry, Marilyn. I have every intention of rescuing him but first we need to get ourselves to a place of safety.'

'What does she mean? What about Carlo?' Sarah looked

round the cabin. 'Where is Carlo?'

'He was taken.'

'Taken? Where?'

'No idea as yet but don't worry. We'll find him, but first we need to get ourselves out of here. I need to have a look in the cockpit.'

'Can you fly this, James?'

'Possibly. If I have to. Come with me, Marilyn. You might be able to show me where things are.'

'I don't think I can.'

'Well you never know so come on. You, too, Mark. Six eyes are better than two. You might spot something I miss.' That wasn't strictly true. James just wanted to get the two of them on their own so he could talk to them without worrying Sarah. She had enough to do, looking after Salvatore. He was dreading what they might find in the cockpit so he made sure he was the first one to go in. He held the door so that Marilyn and Mark couldn't follow him.

Thankfully there were no dead bodies in the cockpit. What James had heard were the kidnappers making sure the plane would never fly again. All the instruments had been shot to smithereens. Everything was ruined including the radio. 'Damn! Damn! Damn!' James muttered to himself. He sat down and considered their predicament. He gazed through the windows. They seemed to be on an old deserted airfield. The runway was fractured with cracks from which grass sprouted. It was a miracle they had landed safely. 'Pilot knew what he was doing.'

'Why d'you say that?' asked Mark.

'There's cracks all over the runway yet we didn't skid or turn over.'

'Oh aye. Lucky or what?'

'See those buildings over there?'

'Yeah. What are they? Houses?'

'No. They're Customs buildings, I think.'

James was suddenly aware of Marilyn crying softly into a tissue and it reminded him that he had some questions to ask her. 'I need some information from you, Marilyn. Listen carefully and answer as best you can. How much of that stuff in Italian did you understand?'

'A little.' She was hyperventilating.

'What's the matter, Marilyn? Are you bothered about Carlo shouting at you?'

'I can't understand why he called me bitch. He's never, ever called me that.' Her eyes were filled with pain.

'For God's sake, it was you who told me he wanted you to keep a British passport. Just think back, Marilyn, will you? And as that's the case, he was just trying to make it look like you were a cheap tart so they wouldn't know you were his wife.'

'Oh yes!' Marilyn sighed with relief.

'Now tell me how they knew I was in the SAS from my passport.'

'They didn't say you were in the SAS. They were talking about us being British subjects. They heard you talking in English when we boarded the plane and they were slightly stumped by your Scottish accent. They thought you were Swedish or Danish or something similar. They hadn't expected anyone to board except for me, Carlo and Salvatore. So when they found the four British passports they thought if they took four British people hostage, the SAS would mount a rescue mission. They were terrified. One of them wanted to kill us all so no one could talk. The others thought that was a very bad idea and that's why one of them hit the man who shot Salvatore.'

'Mmm! So that's what Carlo was trying to tell me. I saw

him give me a funny look just after I heard them say SAS. Anyway, that's good.'

'Why is that good?' Mark asked.

'Because they won't be expecting the SAS to catch up with them so quickly.'

'Well the SAS won't want to get involved just for Carlo, will they?'

'I'm not going to ask the SAS as such. I'm going to get hold of a few of my friends. Ex-SAS same as me. We might all have left the army but we still stick together and whoever asks for help gets it. Just haven't got the means to get in touch as yet. No mobiles. No radio. Don't know where the phones are on this bloody island.'

'How d'you know this is an island?'

'Because as we flew over Cuba we crossed a bit of water.'

'Cuba!' Mark gasped. 'We're on Cuba?'

'Well, not quite. I reckon we're on Isla de la Juventud. In English it means the Isle of Youth. It's the place where Castro was imprisoned in the fifties. Eventually he built an airfield and a sort of university campus and invited kids from communist countries to come and study here. He also got them working on the land, growing grapefruit and lemons. Quite a nice little earner it was. What's the matter, Mark?'

Mark was jiggling about in excitement. '*Treasure Island!*' he exclaimed. 'This damn island is all about pirates. That man Robert Louis Stevenson used this place as the basis for his book. You know: *Treasure Island*. My cousins told me all about it. I've got family in Havana. Been to see them a couple of times.'

James looked at him in amazement tinged with appreciation. Of all the people to get stuck with on this desert island it looked like Mark was going to be the answer to his prayers. 'So you could find your way to Havana and get a message to my friends?'

'Yeah! Easy man! Dead easy!'

'Except,' continued James, slowly, 'I don't think we have enough cash and the bastards took the credit cards with them, didn't they?'

'I've got some money,' Marilyn chipped in. 'I've got loads. Euros, pounds, even US dollars.'

'Where?'

'In a secret compartment in my make-up case. Carlo always insisted I keep it there in case of emergencies.'

Carlo and his emergencies! Again! 'OK. That's good. I think we'll need the dollars. They probably accept those here. But you'd best give Mark some English pounds just in case. I haven't got anything. They took my wallet.'

They watched her lift the inside tray out of her case and then she pulled a flat velvet-covered board from the bottom. Sure enough there was a quantity of notes in the bottom. She counted them out. 'There's five hundred dollars and two hundred pounds. Is that enough?' She looked anxious.

'That'll be enough,' Mark assured her. 'I only need to get over to the mainland and then I can get a lift to Havana. Then my family will help me.'

'Actually, as soon as you get on the mainland, get a taxi.'

'Not many taxis on Cuba. Might have to hitch like everyone else does.'

'OK, you know best. As soon as you reach your family ask them to lend you a mobile phone.' James was writing on a scrap of paper. 'This is Ken Smith's phone number. The last time I saw him was at my wedding to Marilyn on the Cayman Islands. All my mates from the SAS were there. That's why we chose the Caymans. While we were together we concocted a question and answer routine in case any of us ever needed help. So this is what you've got to do. As soon as he answers this number, say these words.' James was scribbling down a series of questions and answers. 'You ask these questions and Ken will give you these answers. If your conversation goes exactly like this, you'll know you're speaking to the right person on a secure line. So then you can give him all the details. Tell him just how bad things are and, when you've finished and this is very important, don't give the mobile back. Just pay for it. You can triple what it's worth. Give your family the real deal. Then hang on to the phone and give it to me when we meet again. I'll have to destroy it. Ken's number is one we all use in an emergency. Nobody else must get to know about it. Burn this note as well.'

'Where do I meet you?'

'You'll have to get a flight back to Florida. Oh hell fire!' James gasped.

'What's the matter?'

'You can't fly from Havana to Florida and if the authorities find us they'll just slap us in jail and no one will ever hear of us again. And all because those bastards took our passports.'

'They didn't take the passports.'

Everyone stared at Marilyn.

'What d'you mean? They didn't take the passports?'

'They meant to, obviously, but they put them in a separate bag to the mobiles and the man holding the bag dropped it when that bastard shot Salvatore. He was standing right next to me and after I'd finished screaming I saw it and kicked it under my chair.'

'My God, Marilyn, you little treasure.' James got up, went over to her and kissed her. 'That one little action may have saved all our lives, Carlo's included.' He looked at Mark. 'You can do it. You can fly from Havana to Florida.'

Mark interrupted him. 'Why can't I fly straight to Washington?'

'Because Florida is the only place where flights from Cuba are allowed to land in America. Soon as you land in Florida, contact Senator Ross and tell him everything.' James wrote on another bit of paper. 'Here's his phone number. Use the borrowed mobile. Hopefully he'll arrange for you to fly from Florida to Washington where you can wait for me. I'm not sure how we can get Salvatore off this island in his condition. Maybe the boys will come in a boat.' James sighed. This whole thing was fraught with danger. 'Just be very careful, Mark.'

'What are you lot going to do while I'm on my way to Havana?'

'Nothing we can do except sit tight and pray that no one saw the plane land and no one comes to investigate. Before you go, I'll get your bag from the cargo hold.'

'How the hell are you going to do that?'

'I can access the hold from up here. There will be a trap door somewhere, probably in the galley, Mark. Come and help me look for it. Marilyn, go back in the cabin. Get those passports and look after Sarah and Salvatore. Give a yell if you see or hear anyone coming. Oh, and one more thing, Mark; I need you to help me move Salvatore. He needs to be more comfortable. We'll put him on one of the sofas.'

'No,' said Marilyn. 'There's a proper bed in this aircraft. It's in the master bedroom; there's a small en-suite in there as well.'

They moved Salvatore and then they found the hatch. James retrieved Mark's bag. He thought he'd leave the others till Mark was on his way. Every minute was vital.

It was just coming up to four o'clock in the afternoon when

Mark left. 'It will be light until at least ten o'clock. If I get a lift to the airport I could be in Havana by then.'

CHAPTER SEVENTEEN

Once Mark had left, James set about finding out how much food and water they had. He'd already noticed some crates in the hold. Further investigation revealed they held bottled water. There was an amazing pile of stuff. Shovels and pickaxes. Big plastic tanks. A couple of small domestic generators. What the hell was Carlo up to? He also found some large torches and the batteries that powered them. Those will come in handy, he thought to himself.

Back in the cabin he asked Marilyn if she could conjure up some food from the galley. 'Don't do any cooking; we don't want anyone to smell it. You can make us a cup of tea but no coffee. That's always a dead give away. Good job none of us smokes.'

'I've only put these out. I didn't think anyone would be very hungry yet.' Marilyn had found some cakes and biscuits and had made some tea.

'How long do you think we're going to be here?' Sarah asked, anxiously.

'First of all, Mark will have to find a main road and hope that someone will come along and give him a lift. If that happens, he might get to the main town by about seven o'clock. There must be either an airport or a ferry service but then again he might have to wait till morning. It's all guesswork. I really don't know when he'll get to Havana but I'm hoping he'll be there by lunchtime tomorrow at the very latest.'

'Then what happens?'

'He'll phone Ken and Ken will contact everyone else and, together, they'll plan some sort of rescue mission. Maybe they'll come in a boat or fly to Havana and hire a car. Oh God. I don't know. Anyway, they'll do something,' he finished, trying not to show how worried he really was.

'We're in a bloody mess, aren't we?' Sarah whispered.

There was no point in beating about the bush. 'Yeah!'

'How are we going to survive?'

'For starters we've got everything we need in this plane. We've got three lavatories and a shower, a fully equipped galley. Salvatore has a comfortable bed to lie on and, in case you haven't noticed, there is even a DVD player. There's also a TV but that won't be much good here because it won't pick up an English signal.'

'But those things won't work while we're on the ground.'

'Yes they will.' Marilyn interjected. 'There is something called an auxiliary power unit that runs off the fuel. No need to look so gob-smacked, James. I'm not the dumb blonde you always thought I was.'

'I never did,' James protested.

'Well, anyway, Carlo told me all about it. We can even have the lights on.'

'No. That's one thing we can't do. We don't want anyone to see us and a strange set of lights coming from a deserted airfield at night might get us some unwelcome visitors.'

'Can we use torches then? There'll be some in the hold.'

'Yes. Good idea as long as we drop the blinds and keep the torches pointed on the floor. It's only if we need to go to the loo in the night. Anyway, you heard what Mark said and I agree with him. It probably will stay light till about ten o'clock.'

Then Sarah asked the question James had been dreading.

'And how are they going to find Carlo?'

'I have no idea.'

A small voice chirped up. 'There's an easy way to find my husband.'

Two pairs of eyes converged on Marilyn.

'We all have tracers.'

'What?' James wrinkled his forehead. 'What the hell do you mean? Tracers?'

Marilyn shrugged. 'I think that's what they're called. Watch this.' She took off one of her shoes and turned the heel slightly to reveal a tiny aperture. There was something inside. 'This is it. A tracer. Somewhere in this plane is a small box that will receive a signal from this, if I switch it on. We've all got one.'

'Don't tell me,' said James, wearily. 'I suppose it's in case you get kidnapped.'

Marilyn nodded her head. 'And there's boxes in our homes in Sicily and Rome and one in each of our cars, but I don't think this signal will stretch as far as that,' she said tearfully, 'so they still won't know about us being kidnapped. So it's no good, is it?'

'It won't be any good for your lot, but it will be perfect for my men when they get here. I can't believe you didn't tell me about this before.'

'I just forgot. Anyway, I had a lot on my mind.'

'So now we've got to find the box. Do you know what it looks like?'

'Oh yes,' she said, happily. 'I remember Carlo showing me just after we were married. They're designed to look like a normal piece of equipment. Like in our cars, they are CD players. And here. . . .' She stopped. 'I'm not sure.' Her eyes filled with tears.

'Look, Marilyn, you'd better stop all this crying lark because otherwise you're going to have bags under your eyes in which you'll be able to carry five pounds of potatoes. In each bag,' he added, trying to cheer her up.

She smiled wanly at his joke. 'OK, James. Let's find the box then.'

It took them hours to find it because it was down in the hold and there was so much stuff to search through. They found it in a crate which, according to the label, contained personal items belonging to Carlo. And there was an instruction book. This gave the distance over which it could operate. James had an idea that this was some sort of private radio-controlled locator beacon. The manufacturer's notes stated that it wasn't intended for use with the international satellite system known as Cospas-Sarsat.

He realized straight away that Carlo must have had this made specially for his own personal use so he didn't have to involve the authorities in his own private business. James knew that there would also be a beacon on the aircraft that could be used to alert the search and rescue organizations. He didn't know if their kidnappers had disabled it but he didn't actually care because he didn't want to alert the rescue services. They'd all spend years in a Cuban jail while the British Government conveniently forgot to negotiate for their release. This little piece of fancy equipment was far more effective and it was exactly what his men would need to find Carlo if he was still within range.

James wondered how Mark was going on. He just hoped that he hadn't sent him out on a wild goose chase and he hoped the authorities didn't latch on to him and interrogate him.

He needn't have worried. Mark was still OK but he'd had to walk quite a long way down what appeared to be a private road. It was obvious that it was no longer used as it was overrun with weeds. He breathed a sigh of relief as he reached a main road although this too was badly maintained, at least by British standards. It had taken him an hour so far, which meant the airfield was about five miles from the road. It was now five o'clock in the afternoon.

He gazed around, taking in as much of the surrounding countryside as he could, looking for landmarks as an aid for Ken Smith. There weren't any. There were a few low ridges in the distance and a mass of vegetation. James had briefed him on using the setting sun as a pointer to the west part of the island. He had said he thought the airfield they were on was close to Nueva Gerona, which was in the north.

He turned right and started what he felt would be a very long walk. At least he was still match-fit. He knew he must keep a note of the time because then Ken would at least be able to work out how far he'd walked.

He'd been walking for about half an hour when he heard a rumbling sound behind him. He was very apprehensive. What if it was a police car, or the army? He turned round and was relieved to see a horse and cart. He made the sign that is recognized the whole world over: he stuck a thumb in the air. The horse slowed and stopped and a cheery, sunburned old chap leaned down and regaled him with a flurry of Spanish.

Mark couldn't understand a word apart from something which sounded like hello or good evening. He remembered what James had told him so long ago and quickly he quoted that universal phrase, 'Manchester United.'

It worked like magic. The man jumped down to shake his hand.

Hell fire, thought Mark. I hope he doesn't think I'm a player. He thought he'd better tell him the truth and quickly. He pretended to bend down with a bat and he did a very good impression of hitting a ball for six. Then he pointed to himself.

'Ha! *Sí*! Cricketer.' The man knew a bit of English. 'Americano?'

'No. English and Jamaican.'

The man shook his hand again, even more vigorously. 'On holiday? Yes?'

'Yes and I need to get to Nueva Gerona. Is this the way?'

The man nodded his head. 'I take you. I go there myself. Please get up.' He climbed back up on to the driving board and gave Mark a hand-up. The only thing to sit on was a hard wooden bench. As they set off, a wonderful sharp smell of lemons followed them. The man was obviously on his way to market with his produce.

He kept up a steady stream of conversation in broken English all the way to Nueva Gerona but it was all about Manchester United. Luckily, thanks to the bit of information James had shared with him and some bits he'd remembered himself, Mark was able to tell him that David Beckham was on loan to AC Milan. He now wanted to stay there but Los Angeles Galaxy were having none of it. The man was very happy to give his opinions on what Beckham should do. Even though his broken English was tricky to follow, Mark spent a very pleasant two hours chatting and it more than made up for a journey sitting on a hard slatted bench.

It transpired the man wanted to get his lemons and grapefruit to market ready for the five o'clock start the following day. He was going to sleep at his brother's house on the outskirts of Nueva Gerona. They arrived there at eight o'clock and Mark had managed to make some mental notes of a few prominent landmarks on the outskirts of the city. The farmer dropped him close to the airport. There was a flight to Havana at nine. Due to the fact that Mark looked like a Cuban Jamaican and the flight was an internal one, the airport officials didn't even ask for his passport. They just waved him through. Once he was in Havana he was unable to get any other sort of transport so he had to walk to his cousin's apartment. He was knocking on the door at eleven o'clock.

Back on the Isle of Youth his friends were still awake. There were no lights on in the cabin for obvious reasons. There was a bit of moonlight, which helped and they had torches now, but James had closed the cabin doors and he intended keeping them closed day and night.

'We won't suffocate, will we?' Sarah asked him apprehensively.

'Maybe you should try not to breathe as much,' James answered, thoughtfully. He laughed at the look on both women's faces. 'I'm joking.'

'How can you joke at a time like this.' Marilyn looked aghast.

'Because that's how a soldier gets through the bad times,' he answered. 'Anyway, as far as the fresh air is concerned, in case you haven't noticed, the air conditioning is still working. It's because of the auxiliary power unit. And that's why we can still flush the lavatories.' James was actually wondering how long that facility would last. He had no way of knowing how much water was in the tanks. Possibly enough for a week. However, down in the hold he'd come across some chemical toilets like the ones used by campers. He had absolutely no idea why Carlo's private jet should have chemical toilets, plus the chemicals to use in them. It was quite bizarre. But they would come in handy if the power and water ran out before they were rescued.

How they got through the night he had no idea but the women gradually fell silent and he assumed they were asleep. He didn't even try to sleep. He stayed awake and on guard. But he knew they'd have to share guard duty soon because even he couldn't stay awake indefinitely. He reckoned they could be there even longer than a week. He had no idea if they would escape detection. He knew there were fishing trips to these islands and it was mostly very rich people who came out here to fish. They were usually the sort of people who could afford to charter a private jet similar to Carlo's. So he hoped no one had bothered about an aircraft like this one, flying low over the island. However, his worst fear was that Salvatore would die and it just wouldn't be right, not after he'd saved Sarah. But there was nothing they could do except wait. Everything depended on Mark.

CHAPTER EIGHTEEN

This was their second day and he was very worried about Salvatore. Hour by hour he was becoming more and more feverish. He asked Marilyn if she would bathe him with cold water in an attempt to keep his temperature down, but he knew it might not work. James knew he would need to take the dressing off, examine the wound and clean it, but first he wanted to go and have a good look round the under-floor cargo area where all their baggage was. Sarah insisted on coming with him but he wasn't keen on her seeing what was down there.

He'd already searched the forward galley and found plenty of useful supplies: dried milk, boxes of teabags, biscuits, small individual chocolate bars to give to the passengers, tins of fruit and cream. Things like lemons and olives for making up cocktails. James wasn't planning on letting anyone have any alcohol and he decided that as soon as possible he'd dump it in the cargo hold.

Sarah was gazing round in disbelief. 'What the hell is all this stuff doing down here?'

James knew she was looking at the spades and ropes and batteries. 'No idea,' he grunted. He had no intention of letting Sarah interrogate him on what Carlo was up to. He had his own ideas and he wasn't going to share them. Better leave well alone. He had an idea though that Sarah had already reached her own conclusions.

After the stint in the hold, he cleaned Salvatore's wound and dressed it again. It was a little inflamed but his fever had eased slightly thanks to Marilyn's hard work. So far James didn't think his life was in danger. Marilyn was keeping his lips moist with bottled water. James told them that from now on, they must drink only bottled water. There was easily enough to last them a month. He'd brought a number of crates of bottled water up from the cargo hold so they had plenty. The water in the aircraft tank could be used for washing or flushing loos, until it ran out.

The days and nights passed. During the day they talked about all sorts of stuff. James was trying to keep Sarah and Marilyn calm. He and Sarah discussed the business and agreed that it would be ticking over all right. His mother was used to being in charge when he was away. He asked Sarah how her father would manage.

'He'll be fine. When my mother died it was such a shock.'

James asked gently, 'What happened to your mother? You never actually told me.'

'She had a heart attack. It was so sudden. My father found her in the garden. She'd been there a while and it was too late to help her. He took it much worse than me. I was so wrapped up in my own misery: it was only a year after Tony was killed.'

James let her talk because he thought it might keep her mind off the mess they were in. It was keeping his mind occupied as well and he concentrated on her tale.

'After I found out what Tony had done, I threw myself into my work. I became very self-centred because of Tony. By the time Mum died, I'd built myself a protective shell. Then I realized that my father was sinking fast. I felt so guilty. I knew I had to do something, so I told him about Tony and I pretended I couldn't go on in the business anymore. He rallied round and he started helping me and without either of us noticing, he was suddenly running things and I was able to concentrate on my designs. We got bigger, with the result you see now. Large factory, big design team, directors and board members. My father is enjoying himself running things and even though we sometimes have the odd disagreement, he's usually right, like he was about you. It seems a lifetime since I picked you up at the airport.'

'Talking about airports, you remember when you flew off to Rome and I went looking for you? When I couldn't find you, I hired a private detective.'

'I know. Mark blurted it out in Arlington Cemetery. It was very sweet of you. We thought we were so much in love.'

'I did love you and I always will, Sarah. But I love you because we've been friends for such a long time and that love will never change.'

'Thank you, James, and I will always love you too.' Sarah suddenly realized that James might not get a chance to marry Sandra unless they got away from Cuba safely. She changed the subject quickly. 'So the detective told you where I was?'

'Well he tracked you as far as Palazzo Vasari.' James just stopped himself repeating what John Parker had told him. Better not add fuel to the fire.

'If it hadn't been for Marilyn and Carlo I would have been alone in Rome.'

'Marilyn's turned out all right. I used to think she was a bit dizzy. She only seemed to care about clothes and make-up.'

'It was her job, James. She was a model and a damned good one.'

'Yes, I know, but she used to drive me mad. Whenever we went away she used to take everything including the kitchen sink. Honest to God, she could have gone door to door, flogging her own cosmetics.'

'Well I guess we should be thankful that she's never lost the habit.'

Marilyn had provided them with baby wipes, facial wipes, camomile lotion when the heat made their skin prickle, talcum powder, deodorant, tissues and when Sarah trapped her finger in the lavatory door, she even produced some witch hazel.

But Sarah had more to thank Marilyn for. She was helping James look after Salvatore. She hadn't even asked Sarah if she wanted to take a turn watching over him. James had gently shaved him because no one wanted to see the thick stubble that kept on growing even though he was unconscious. It was as though they all wanted to preserve the real Salvatore so he wouldn't slip away. Sarah was glad they hadn't asked her to do anything for him as she knew she couldn't bear to touch him. It was breaking her heart because she knew she couldn't possibly marry into a family that had connections with the Mafia. And after what she'd seen down in the hold, she knew without a shadow of a doubt that Carlo's family were in with the Sicilian Mafia and that's how they could afford this private jet. It had all become very clear. No wonder they had so many bodyguards.

On the fourth day, they heard a plane fly over. James didn't say anything but it seemed like the plane was flying pretty low. Having a look at them, maybe? He sincerely hoped it wasn't. When James had said that they would be rescued within a week he knew he was wrong. It was an impossible task. And on the sixth day when they heard the rumble of what sounded like several trucks, James knew that whoever was flying the plane must have seen them and alerted the authorities. He knew it was far too soon for his men to have arrived. His heart was pounding. The game was up. His last thought was, at least they had their passports. Then there was a tremendous banging on the cabin door. Reluctantly he opened it.

Ken Smith was first in, clutching his old buddy to his chest and pummelling him hard on the back. Another four men followed him. They were the ones whom James had served with in the SAS.

'How did you get here so quick?' James gasped.

'We flew to the Caymans and an American destroyer picked us up. Apparently a bloke called Senator Ross organized it.' Suddenly more men dived in. 'This lot insisted on coming to shake your hand, James.' Ken was exuberant.

James looked totally confused.

One of the men spoke. He had an American accent. 'We wanted to pay our respects to the man who brought Major Jamie Ross home.'

'How do you know about that? You can't be old enough to know him.'

'Well, sir,' the man drawled, 'it's all gone down in the history of the regiment. What you did, sir, is considered to be a supreme act of bravery. Everyone knows the name of the Scottish soldier who stayed by the body of one of our comrades. We might not be able to give medals to the men of the SAS but we can be ready to help them whenever they need help. Put it there, sir.' He held out his hand.

Suddenly the other Americans were crowding round and shaking hands with James. He was overwhelmed by it all.

Sarah and Marilyn flung their arms round one another, in floods of tears.

'Say! I hear you've got an injured man?' One of the soldiers was carrying a medical bag. 'OK if I examine him, sir?'

'I'll be glad if you do,' said James. 'I've done what I can but you'll see it's not much. He's been unconscious since he was shot. He's got a fever. I left the bullet in. We've put him on the bed in the master bedroom.'

Salavatore was still motionless, undisturbed by all the celebrations.

'Hmm!' the medic grunted. 'You did exactly the right thing.' He taped the dressing back. 'I'll give him a shot of morphine then we can get him into the truck. Best thing is to get him back to our ship where we can do some emergency surgery. We'll get the bullet out. We've been instructed to fly him to Walter Reed in Washington. Some senator has been in touch with the top brass.'

He was referring to the Walter Reed Army Medical Center. There was no better medical facility in the world, but it was reserved for the military. Senator Ross must have really leaned on someone to get Salvatore in there. 'How did you all get here so quickly?' As he was asking the question his eyes were following the Americans who were darting up and down the cabin placing what looked like detonators.

'Never mind the questions. We need to get you off Cuba before anyone finds us. You've been pretty lucky so far.'

'Yes, I know. A plane flew over two days ago, having a look, I think.'

'Sorry sir. That was us. We wanted to get your position. Anyway, better get going folks.'

The Americans looked like they were in charge. Salvatore was strapped on to a stretcher and lowered carefully down to the ground. Then he was lifted into one of the vehicles standing on the runway. It was a thirty-year-old Dodge with a cab at the front for the driver and up to two passengers. The back was open to the elements and there was a long bench down each side. There was plenty of room for Salvatore to be laid on the floor, at their feet, between the benches. James pointed out which bags they needed to take with them, including a bag containing the precious radio equipment that he hoped would track Carlo. When they set off down the runway, James could see that the other Dodge hadn't moved.

The American leader of the mission, who had introduced himself as Glenn, saw James looking. 'They won't be long. Just making sure that when anyone finds your plane they won't have the slightest idea where it's come from. Won't be much left.'

James asked him what they were using.

Glenn told him. Then he said, 'Enough to turn the whole aircraft into dust.'

At last the second truck came trundling after them.

'There will be a nice little firework display in three hours' time. We'll be out at sea by then. No one will know what the hell's happened there.'

Since they hadn't had any unwelcome visitors for nearly a week, James was pretty confident that no one would be near enough to get blasted to kingdom come.

Glenn read his expression. 'Don't worry. I shouldn't be telling you this, but a couple of my boys are staying behind. They've positioned themselves on top of those Custom buildings. They should be able to see for miles. If they see anyone in the distance they'll detonate the lot straight away just to be on the safe side. Then they'll disappear. Their families are from Puerto Rico so they speak Spanish. They won't look out of place. They'll get back to the US of A under their own steam.' He laughed and added, 'Eventually!'

'Now, ladies, I have something to say to you and I don't want you to take it the wrong way or get embarrassed. If we run into any security folk I want you to act like you're a couple of hookers. Just pretend you're having a good time. My boys will have to mess about a bit and they'll have to kiss you. Putting it politely; the Cubans are a pretty affectionate race. Must be all that dancing in the streets. Just take it in your stride and try and put on a convincing act. Pity you're both blonde but they'll probably think you're a couple of American tourists out for a good time. Mind you, my boys don't look much like Cubans either. That could be a problem. And then we have this body as well, we might have to throw some of our clothes over him. It's all a bit risky so let's just hope no one stops us.'

Marilyn and Sarah were starting to look pretty nervous.

'Don't worry. We probably won't see anyone. I guess I just don't like the fact that we've got to travel in an open pick-up but we needed something that wouldn't stand out in a country where all the cars date back to the sixties.'

'I thought your military had stopped using these,' James commented.

'They have. They were phased out over ten years ago. But we always know where to get hold of a few for a clandestine op like this one. We were also told we'd got a stretcher case to pick up and this old Dodge is perfect for that. But I'm afraid it's pretty uncomfortable.'

'Where are we headed?' James asked him.

'A place called Colony. It's not what you'd call a hot spot for tourists. But it's like heaven on earth to a scuba diver. There's a fancy hotel there that's devoted to the sport. I think they actually have a fleet of taxis, though fleet might be a bit of an exaggeration. I think there are two. But they've also laid on stuff like medical services for diving emergencies. It's a real global magnet for divers hence the stuff that we're loaded up with. Thought we could blend in with all this diving equipment. We picked Colony because even though it's popular with the diving fraternity, it's not popular with the ordinary tourist being pretty difficult to get here. Hopefully no one will be interested in us. We've got a dinghy moored there. She's made from glass-fibre reinforced plastic. Sorry. Here I am, giving you a lecture. I expect you've been in one of those plenty of times. Anyway she's painted to look like an old wooden fishing boat. She looks pretty beat up but under her disguise she's a real fast lady. A few of my men are sailing her in and out, trying to make it look as though they're going on a few dives. So that's where we're headed and I've already informed my lads over the radio that we've found you. There's a much bigger boat lying out in international waters ready to give assistance. And if there's any trouble they'll send a couple of helicopters out to get us. Hope we don't need them because it'll probably cause an international incident.'

Obviously a destroyer is sitting out there, thought James. And they must have ferried the old pick-up trucks in. 'I've got something to show you that might change things for me and my boys. I've lost one of my party but he's got a small personal transmitter on him.' He unzipped his bag and took out the radio-controlled locator.

'Mmm! Interesting.'

'Apparently all Carlo's family carry a locator beacon built into one heel of every pair of shoes. When no one is watching, all they have to do is, slip a shoe off and activate the signal, which is received by this box. The trouble is I'm not exactly sure of the range. I tried for a signal as soon as I found it but there wasn't one. I think Carlo's had these specially made. The manual stated they weren't for use with Cospas-Sarsat. And it all depends if Carlo has had the opportunity to set it off without being seen. He might not have been able to take his shoe off.'

'So I take it you and your boys won't want to leave this

island till you've done a sweep. You've set yourselves a difficult task, James.'

'Yep. I know.'

'It strikes me these friends you've hitched up with are not quite kosher. I mean, there's this one with a bullet in him. Don't you think you'd be better off pulling out now and forgetting about the other one?'

'Oh no!' Marilyn cried out.

'Calm down, Marilyn, I'm not leaving Carlo. Look, mate, this chap here,' he pointed to Salvatore, 'saved my fiancée's life. He threw himself in front of her to stop a bullet and he was expecting to be killed. So I reckon I owe him one. As it happens he wasn't killed, but the gunmen took his brother. I can repay him by rescuing Carlo. You of all people should understand. It's a debt of honour. And the man they've taken is Marilyn's husband – Marilyn is my ex-wife.' He'd deliberately lied about Sarah being his fiancée but she'd had the sense not to challenge him.

'Well, James, don't you lead a complicated life? But I see where you're coming from and now I know the details I'll give you all the help I can. I need to get on my radio and organize another boat. We'll stay behind and give you a hand. Gives us another chance to say thanks for bringing a soldier back to his regiment and his family. That's a debt that will never be fully repaid and it'll give us a chance to work with your special forces even if they're a bunch of, what d'ya call 'em over in England? Old-age pensioners?'

The ex-SAS men, who were listening, bristled up.

James just laughed. 'I reckon we can give you a run for your money.'

'In the meantime, now we're on the road to freedom, I suggest you turn on that little box of tricks just in case your friend is hanging out round here. It might be that the kidnappers have also used Colony as their base. They would have wanted to evade the authorities in this part of the world same as we're trying to do.'

James didn't have much hope that he was right, but all the same he took Glenn's advice and turned on the receiver. He only hoped that if Carlo was close by, the battery in his personal locator was still working. He thought it ought to be, but on the other hand, it had been nearly a week since he'd been taken away.

CHAPTER NINETEEN

The two big trucks lumbered their way twenty-six miles south-west to the scuba diving resort of Colony. They'd been on the road for about twenty minutes when there was a faint pinging sound from the receiver.

Marilyn looked up. 'Is that. . . ?'

'Yeah, but don't start getting excited.' He hated saying it but he had to prepare her for the worst. 'They could have removed his shoes.'

'What on earth for?'

'I don't know, do I?' Or Carlo could be dead and they've dumped the body, he thought to himself. He couldn't bring himself to say the words aloud but he saw Sarah look at him and he knew she was thinking the same thing.

The nearer they got to Colony, the stronger the signal became. Glenn struggled from his seat at the front of the truck, edging round Salvatore, to where James was sitting at the back. 'Is that a signal? Was I right or was I right?' He looked smug.

'Yeah, but before we get too excited I need a word with you, on the quiet. Is there anywhere we can pull over?'

'Hang on. I'll go and have a word with the driver. Good job we're in the front truck. The other driver will see us pulling in.' He went back to the front and banged on the back window. 'Tell Pete to look out for some sort of pull-in. Something's come up.'

A few minutes later the truck slowed down, swerved to the right and stopped.

Marilyn looked worried. 'Why are we stopping?'

'I need to have a word with Glenn. I want you and Sarah to stay here with Salvatore.' Then he called to four of his men, 'Jack, Ken, Adam, Jon – I want a word with you. Eric! Stay with the girls.' He jumped down on to the road and the four men followed him.

Glenn had already got over the side of the truck at the front end and was waiting on the grassy verge. The other truck was just grinding to a halt and a soldier got down from the passenger seat and joined them. 'What's up?'

'Not sure, Rob. James needs to talk to his men. Look, you get back in the truck and be ready to drive off at a minute's notice.' The soldier went back to his truck and Glenn looked enquiringly at James.

'You know I've got this signal and it's getting stronger. Well, I'm worried about what sort of shape Carlo might be in when we find him. He might even be dead and I don't want the women hanging on my coat tails when we go looking for him, even if he's close to Colony. So what I want your men to do' – he looked at Glenn – 'is to grab the women and get them off this island pronto.'

Glenn drawled, 'I couldn't have put it better. Been thinking along the same lines myself.'

The ex-SAS men nodded in agreement.

'They won't like it and you might have a bit of a fight on your hands, particularly with his wife, Marilyn. You'll just have to use a bit of force if necessary, but whatever you have to do, get them off this island together with Salvatore. If we don't have them to worry about, the boys and I will work a lot better.'

'Yep! I agree. By the way, I'm leaving you four of my boys.'

'We don't need them,' Ken Smith cut in. 'We can manage on our own.'

'I have absolutely no doubt you can, but a few Americans might come in handy when you want a ride back. And we know our way round Cuba better than you lot. We've been here quite a while you know. Don't worry. I've told my men that when I've gone, James will be in charge. Now, let's get this show on the road before someone comes along and spots us parked up like this.'

They arrived in Colony and parked the trucks behind some bushes hoping they would stay hidden until the operation was over. They would be left behind. Two dinghies were at anchor in a quiet part of the bay, well away from a small pier, which looked like it belonged to the hotel. As soon as the trucks were parked up safely, the Americans had a look round to make sure no one was watching. Then they waded out to one of the dinghies, carrying Salvatore as carefully as possible. At the same time another two of the ex-SAS men helped the Americans with the women. They were manhandled into the same dinghy. Marilyn started arguing, but one of the men put a hand over her mouth and pointed to the hotel. She got the message, but James knew she'd be furious and she'd give him a real earful when they met up again. He wasn't bothered. If he was being honest with himself, he was just glad to see the back of them. It wouldn't be long before they were safely in the hands of the American Navy. Thank God for that!

The four Americans, who had been left behind, waited for instructions from James. They knew that from now on he was leader of this rescue mission and they trusted him. Dress was casual; torn jeans and grubby T-shirts courtesy of the US Navy.

'Right. Let's get over to that.' He pointed to a boathouse about a quarter of a mile down the beach. It was in a very dilapidated state but it was exactly the sort of place he wanted. 'We need a plan of action.'

They reached the boathouse and slipped inside. It was empty and looked as though no one had been there for years.

'OK, Ken, let's think about this. There are four permutations: either Carlo is here alone; Carlo is here and he's dead; they've taken his shoes off and dumped them, but I don't think that's likely; or Carlo is here and so are our little friends. So we have to find out where this signal is coming from and try and spring a surprise.'

'Boss, I reckon we should wait till it's dark,' said Ken Smith. He was a tall good-looking man with red hair and muscles like Arnold Schwarzenegger. 'We stand a better chance of creeping up on these fellas at night.'

'What happens if the battery on that tracer runs out and the signal ceases?'

'It doesn't really matter. We'll still know he's in the vicinity.'

'I reckon a couple of us should have a scout round,' said Ken. 'See if we can spot any strange comings and goings. You'd think that if they're hanging about for a boat, they'll need sustenance. Food and alcohol, I should think. Might see 'em coming back from the hotel bar.'

'Good idea. So me and you then?'

'Why you?'

'Because I know what they look like.'

'Oh aye! Great idea!' Ken scowled. 'You know what they look like! And they don't know what you look like? Why don't I take my little brother?'

Adam Smith glowered at him. He was just as big and muscular as Ken.

'Ah! Mmm! Good point. OK, take Adam. No one will connect a couple of boys with red hair and Lancashire accents to me.'

'Well, hopefully, we won't be having any sort of conversation with 'em so our accents don't matter, you plonker.'

'OK! OK! Point taken. Just don't be long; we'll be having something to eat shortly. And for Christ's sake, keep out of trouble.'

The sun was setting. It reminded him of that sunset on Sicily when he arrived at the Villa Vallerina and found Sarah looking so dishevelled. He grinned as he realized he must have interrupted them at a fairly emotional moment. He was sure that Sarah loved Salvatore and her rejection of marriage hadn't fooled him one bit. He wondered why she was in denial. Maybe she didn't want to live in Sicily. Maybe she thought it was too far away from her father. After what Salvatore had done for Sarah, James was pretty certain that the Sicilian would go and live anywhere in the world with her.

There was a scrambling sound behind the boathouse. All the men jumped up and positioned themselves near the double doors.

Someone started whistling outside. James recognized the tune and he opened one of the doors. Ken and Adam slipped in silently. James shut the door quickly.

'Well?'

Ken looked pleased with himself. 'Found 'em all right. Heard 'em talking. There's another of these boathouses about two miles up the beach. Looks like they've been using it as a hide out. Must be waiting for a boat or something. Might be that something's gone wrong with their timetable, or the authorities have spotted their boat coming into the bay and they've scarpered. They didn't sound very happy. They were muttering away in Italian.'

In the end, James had decided to send his men out without the receiver, on the grounds that it would alert anyone who heard it pinging. So now he hardly dared ask the question. 'Did you see Carlo?'

'Nope. Sorry, mate. Couldn't see anything. Didn't want to mess about outside for too long. Didn't want to attract their attention.'

'Yeah. Quite right.' James hid his disappointment. 'Here help yourself to these cold hot dogs.'

Everyone laughed.

'I don't believe I just said that! Well,' he said defiantly, 'we can't heat them up but they taste bloody good. There are some cold beans and they taste great. Some dry biscuits as well. It's all thanks to our new friends. They've brought some energy drinks. No beer, I'm afraid.' He grinned at them. 'Gotta keep our brains in gear. We'll be getting out there tonight'

There were ten men. Six ex-SAS soldiers and four Americans from Delta Force. They hadn't actually said they were part of that elite organization but James knew they were just by looking at them. For a start they all had fairly long hair, nothing like the usual short back and sides that was the only thing permitted in the services. He knew that the kidnappers wouldn't stand a chance against ten very fit and extremely well-trained soldiers.

They moved quietly through the gloom. It was midnight. They hoped their quarry would be asleep and even if they weren't they wouldn't be expecting a raid. It was a week since they'd left the plane and they probably thought the rest of their victims had died or were close to death. What a surprise they were going to get.

James and his rescue task force burst into the boathouse and three of the Americans switched on the searchlights they were carrying. The men inside were blinded. All hell broke out, but within minutes the gangsters were laid out unconscious, securely tied up and gagged.

James cast a glance round the floor and spotted a large hump under a dirty blanket. His heart was in his mouth as he strode over, closely followed by Ken. Carlo was out cold. James felt for a pulse. He was alive, but he was in a very bad state. He turned round and went back to the kidnappers, lying on the floor, trussed up like turkeys ready for the oven. He kicked them into consciousness.

'You're just lucky my mate's alive. If he'd been dead, I would be executing the lot of you, right now. As it is, once we're well away from this beach, we'll pass a message to the Cubans that you're here. Of course, when they come for you, you might wish I had topped you.' And then he gave them something else to think about because he knew he'd never see them again 'When you were talking in our plane, you thought the SAS were going to come looking for you. Well you didn't realize how true that was because it was an SAS man that you kidnapped. Me!' He was pleased to see fear spreading over their faces, but since he wasn't a man who killed in cold blood, they were going to live, although they might be living in a Cuban jail for a while.

One of the Americans had a look at Carlo. 'He ain't gonna make it unless we can get him out to the ship ASAP. We ain't waiting for the morning; we go tonight, folks. We'll have to use that blanket. Pity we only brought one stretcher.'

The four Americans took over. They loaded Carlo on to the

blanket, which they had already knotted in all four corners as a makeshift stretcher and carried it the three miles to the dinghy politely refusing all offers of assistance from the ex-SAS men, who seemed to know that it was something to do with honour. James knew they were carrying Carlo for him and for the men who had carried Jamie twenty miles through the dense jungle. He thanked God it wasn't twenty miles tonight.

They lifted him into the dinghy. The boat was about fifteen feet long and was quite large enough for all of them. Some of the men from Delta Force, helped by the ex-SAS men, picked up the oars and started rowing softly and skilfully till they were a few hundred yards from the shore. Then they shipped the oars and raised the sails.

'We've got an outboard motor but we think silence is better than speed now.

One of the men was speaking quietly into a radio. Then he turned to James and said the magic words. 'Won't be long before we get picked up.' And he was right. Half an hour later they were all being loaded on to a US naval destroyer. Carlo was carried away to the hospital wing. James thanked everyone. The men from Delta Force looked embarrassed because they just thought they'd done their duty, but James told them he was going to be forever in their debt.

Carlo recovered quite quickly. When he was well enough he told James that the men, having failed to get him back in the fold, had intended to try for some ransom money. They knew Carlo's family would pay up and that's why they hadn't killed him. But then something went wrong with their lift home. James also heard some other interesting stuff. Carlo swore him to secrecy. James wasn't too happy, but in the end he gave in.

When Carlo was stable he was put in a helicopter with

James and his men and they were flown to Washington. By the time they got there Salvatore was also on his way to making a complete recovery, thanks to what had been done for him on board the naval vessel.

At last it was time to go home. They were flown back in another private jet, courtesy of the US Army and Senator Ross. Landing in Rome, they all left the plane in order to watch the soldiers bring Salvatore down the ramp. Just as a precaution, they placed him in a wheelchair.

'That wheelchair could have been a body-bag,' Mark muttered to James.

'That wheelchair could have been six body-bags,' James whispered back. 'We're all lucky to be alive. And a lot of it is thanks to you, mate.'

They all walked over to Salvatore. Mark and James said their goodbyes quickly and went back up the steps into the plane.

Carlo kissed Sarah and then he took a few steps backwards and waited.

Sarah was left with Marilyn and Salvatore, the man who had saved her life.

'Time to say goodbye, Sarah.' He said the words defiantly almost as if he knew without being told he'd lost out to James, but nothing could be further from the truth.

Sarah had told James that she would never marry Salvatore and that it was over between them. And that was the truth. But she was now going to tell Salvatore that she was back with James and that was a lie. The truth for James and a lie for Salvatore? How could she do it? Then she looked into his eyes and saw it wasn't necessary. She also knew that she would never, ever stop loving him. She would never forget he had saved her life. And standing on that runway in Rome she made a silent vow that she would never marry anyone else because she knew she could never forget Salvatore Vasari. She would spend the rest of her life alone. It was a fair price to pay to the man who had made sure she would live that life. She bent and kissed him for the last time.

He took hold of her hands and said something. But it was all in Sicilian and she didn't understand a word of it. Then he let go of her hands. Carlo stepped forward and took hold of the wheelchair. Suddenly Salvatore was gone out of her life for ever. She watched Carlo take him to the car that would carry him safely back to the family home.

Bewildered, she stared at Marilyn. 'I don't suppose you know what he said?'

'Oh yes,' said Marilyn. 'The words of love are easy for me to understand. I can quote it exactly. "I shall love you forever, my darling. Now and forever farewell". So, Sarah, I simply cannot understand how you can let him go.' And Marilyn burst into tears and walked blindly away.

Sarah bent her head and the dam burst. The tears spilled down her cheeks, on to the tarmac and so that Marilyn wouldn't see she was crying, she too turned away. She stumbled up the steps and into the cabin.

CHAPTER TWENTY

James and Sandra were finally getting married. Sandra had told James that she wanted to get married in Scotland. Everyone was absolutely delighted including the senator and his wife. As far as they were concerned, Scotland was the most romantic place in the universe. They were going to stay at a fabulous hotel near Dornoch and they were both hoping to get in some rounds of golf at the famous Royal Dornoch Golf Club.

They were staying for a month so they could tour the whole of Scotland. They wanted to see everything. The list was endless and it wasn't all close together either. They wanted to see Loch Lomond, Glencoe, John o' Groats and, most definitely, the Loch Ness monster. James said he and Sandra would go with them and they would take Jamie as well. He knew all the best beaches; the most incredible lochs, the most spectacular mountains and he was going to make sure that they took as many beautiful memories as possible back to Washington.

And then when the senator's family flew back to Washington, James was taking Sandra on a Mediterranean cruise. 'Just so we can get a bit of sun.' They looked all set for a wonderful life together at last.

Sarah looked round the church. She was sitting next to her father on the groom's side. Behind were Jane, her husband and three daughters, Lizanne, Bettina and Amy. Lizanne had been working at Living Stones. She had stepped ably into Sarah's shoes while she was away in Sicily. She was a fabulously talented designer who had just obtained a First in jewellery design at Goldsmiths. Mark's wife Pam was sitting next to Lizanne. Sarah was very fond of Jane's daughters. They all called her Aunty Sarah and it gave her a feeling of belonging to a large warm-hearted family. This time, James had picked Neil Anderson as his Best Man. Mark and Ken were showing everyone to their seats. Sandra's two sisters were bridesmaids.

Jane had gone mad when Sarah told her James and Sandra were getting married.

'Oh my God! I can't believe James is doing this to you. You were so in love with one another. How on earth can he be marrying someone else? What? What?'

Sarah was laughing at her. When she explained everything Jane was silent for a few moments.

'But that leaves you on your own again. That's not fair.'

'That's life, Jane,' Sarah replied sadly.

When Jane found out Maurice Cresson was coming to the wedding and that he was single, fancy-free, very rich and, according to Sarah, drop-dead gorgeous, she started making plans to fix up Sarah with him.

'He's too old for me and I don't want to live in France.' It was just an excuse because Sarah didn't believe that age was a factor when you fell in love. But it was true that she didn't want to live in France. She wanted to live in Sicily but she didn't tell Jane and she hadn't told her anything about Salvatore either.

'OK. So what about the Best Man? He's supposed to be

sweet on you and he's nice looking and he's Scottish, like James.'

'Who told you all that and who told you Neil was sweet on me?'

'Elizabeth.'

Sarah made a mental note to steer clear of Neil. In fact, she knew it wouldn't matter if Tom Cruise were at the wedding: she wasn't interested in romance or love or even dating men anymore. She just hoped she could keep Neil Anderson at arm's length. He was a nice man but he just didn't appeal to her. It had been a year since she had seen Salvatore but her feelings for him were just as strong.

Everywhere she looked there were reminders, although she didn't need them. Not a day went by that he didn't fill her thoughts. Every morning as soon as she woke up she wondered where he was. At the end of every day, she stared out of the window and pretended she was back in his arms. In spite of the fact that she was so unhappy, she forced herself to work. The strange thing was, she was doing the best designs she had ever done in her life.

'Wow! Aunty Sarah, I love these reds and yellows and the way you've slipped these dark orange stones in between. They blend so perfectly with these turquoises.' Lizanne was obviously impressed. 'I wish I were as talented as you. Who would have thought these colours would look so good, together?'

'Try looking at the sunset each evening.'

'These aren't quite the same colours as the sunset, are they?' Lizanne sounded puzzled. 'Aren't they a bit too vivid?'

'Yes. I suppose you're right. These colours are more like a Mediterranean sunset. Actually they remind me of the sunsets in Sicily. They are the most beautiful sunsets in the world.' Sarah's voice grew distant and dreamy. She was far,

far away and she was talking to herself. 'A Sicilian sunset is designed by the gods themselves.'

'What gods, Aunty Sarah?'

But Sarah realized she'd said too much and she darted out of the office.

Later, Lizanne told her mother, 'You'd think she was in love, the way she was behaving. She was in a dream but I've never seen such inspired designs.'

'Maybe that holiday did her good.'

'You don't think she met someone there, do you?'

'No, I shouldn't think so. She would have told me.'

Lizanne wasn't the only one who was puzzled by Sarah's behaviour. Kevin Jones, her part-time gardener, had also found himself wondering what was wrong with her.

Sarah had been wandering aimlessly round the garden. It was the beginning of October and James was getting married in two weeks' time. It had been raining all summer, but at the moment the weather was warm and balmy. Everyone had been saying what a rotten summer it had been. She was fed up with hearing about summer. No one could have had a worse summer than she'd had. In fact, the whole year had been horrible. It was a year since she'd seen Salvatore. A year of pain and misery.

The months had passed her by and here she was back in a garden where the flowers were fading fast again. But she was beginning to notice things at last. She noticed for the first time that her roses had suffered badly this year. There were hardly any leaves on them and most of the buds were bloated with rain and squelchy to the touch. But a few had stood up to the weather. There was a new patio rose called Warm Welcome. Its open orange petals gleamed in the rays from the setting sun. It was a beautiful little rose but all it did was remind her that there was no warm welcome waiting for her when she returned from work each day and there never would be.

The vibrant red petals of Altisimo called to her. That had also stood up to the weather. Was that an Italian name? Maybe not. She turned her back on it and there was her favourite: Nightlight. It had started off as a tight orange bud, opened, turned deep gold and now it was tinged with blood red. It reminded her of a Sicilian sunset. She knew if she as much as touched one petal, every part of it would fall to the ground. Hesitantly she put out a hand.

'They all need dead-heading, Mrs Livingstone.' A voice intruded into her dreams. The gardener advanced with his secateurs.

'Oh! No!' she gasped. 'Don't do that.'

But it was too late. His hand shot out, grasped the rose before the petals could fall untidily on to the ground and, snip! Into the collecting bag with the rest, it went. Kevin Jones stared in consternation at Sarah as she burst into tears.

'Mrs Livingstone. Whatever's the matter? There are plenty more buds to come. See? Look at this lovely pale-yellow one, just starting to open.'

'Yes, I know, but the other one looked just like the sunset, with all those different colours on the same flower.'

The gardener stared at her. What on earth was she talking about? Looked like the sunset? Barmy! She was a very nice lady but since losing Mr Livingstone in that dreadful plane crash, she'd been a bit unpredictable. But he still liked her and he tried to make allowances for her.

'I'm sorry. Everything's been getting on top of me, lately. I'm just being daft. Of course you have to dead-head all the roses.'

'Not all, Mrs Livingstone.' He spoke firmly but gently, in the same patient tone of voice that he used for his grandchildren. 'I always leave the ones that are going to have nice red hips so they are nice for you to look at in winter.'

'Thank you, Kevin.' She touched him gently on the arm and then she left him to his task. He'd said the hips would be nice to look at in winter. Winter! It was nearly here. Again! It was autumn already. A whole year without the man she loved. She stared round the garden. All the trees were turning red and gold and copper and deep yellow. Even the trees reminded her of the evenings she had spent with Salvatore. Her heart ached for him.

She went inside and turned on the radio. Frank Sinatra was crooning an old favourite. What a bastard life was. Viciously her finger bounced on and off the button. Silence! The stand-by light blinked at her offensively. The words of the song still echoed in her broken heart. She would always miss him. And when the leaves, drifting past her window, were all the colours of a Sicilian sunset, how could she ever forget Salvatore Vasari?

She went to her bedroom. The small bottle of men's cologne was sitting on her dressing-table. She sat down on the small boudoir chair. The bottle tantalized her. She took off the top and sprayed her arms with it. She had searched and searched for his cologne in the shops but had been unable to find the right one. She had tried every Italian cologne she could find on display. She could see the assistants muttering to each other every time they saw her. She'd been in about twenty different shops in Manchester and by now they all knew her; it was obvious they thought she was a nutcase.

Eventually she had to resort to searching the web. She finally found a fantastic site where you could enter the names of what they called the perfume notes and the site would find the nearest match. The best thing was, you could enter a combination of the notes. She had entered the words cedar and patchouli and it had come up with a match: more than one, in fact. She'd sent for four. She knew it was madness but she could always give them away as presents and she did. All except for one.

The nearest match now sat here on her dressing-table. The bottle was neat: a narrow cube with a black and silver top. Silver Shadow by Davidoff. It was that timeless, ocean-fresh smell that followed Salvatore around. The reason she hadn't been able to find this one in the shops was because it wasn't Italian. She suspected that it wasn't the one he used but it smelt exactly how she remembered.

She felt guilty every time she used it because she knew it had become an obsession. She wondered if it was the same as being addicted to sniffing glue. Her insides curled up in horror. She needed to get a grip. Lots of people were addicted to perfume. It wasn't a sin to love something beautiful. Something that made you feel good couldn't be a sin. The trouble was, it didn't make her feel good. She went to sleep at night bathed in the stuff and had the most wonderful dreams of being in his arms again. But she always woke up with tears running down her cheeks. This wasn't good for her, she knew. Maybe if she talked to Jane. No! Jane would just drag her off to a psychiatrist. Sarah hadn't told Jane about the kidnapping. It had been decided by everyone who was involved that there were too many complications and too many things which could still get them all into trouble. So no one was saying anything about it. As far as Jane and Elizabeth and Sarah's father were concerned, James had taken everyone to see Jamie's grave. And that was all. It was safer that way; for everyone.

All James's army friends were at his wedding and they had brought their wives. They had chosen to sit on the bride's side, to make up the numbers. Sandra's mother was there, but her father had died some years previously. She had invited a few of her cousins but having lived in the USA for so long meant she'd lost touch with her friends. The senator and his wife were sitting on her side. Her son Jamie was giving her away and looked very handsome in his cadet uniform.

It was a beautiful service and the reception was in full swing when James came to find Sarah. He grabbed her by the arm and pulled her away from the group of people to whom she was talking.

'Ouch. You're hurting me. What d'you think you're doing?' His fingernails were like needles digging into her upper arm. The pain was excruciating.

James loosened his grip slightly but he still dragged her into the next room where all the wedding presents were on display. 'Here! Look!'

'What?'

'Look!'

'Wedding presents. So what? What d'you want me to say?'

'I want you to look at the message on this one.'

'Ah! It's from Carlo, Marilyn and Salvatore. Well? So what?' She stared at him.

'It's not who it's from, you idiot! It's who it's to. Look again, Sarah.'

'Ooops! That's a bit dodgy.' She giggled. 'You'd better get rid of that before Sandra sees it.' The note was brief and it appeared Marilyn had written it: *Dear James, just a little gift for you and Sarah. Sorry we can't be there. We're packing as I speak. Love and kisses. From Marilyn, Carlo and Salvatore.*

'Why on earth did you tell them you were marrying me?'

Sarah shook her head and protested, 'I never did any such thing. I haven't spoken to them since we left them in Rome. Anyway, why didn't you tell them you were getting married to Sandra and not me?'

'Mmm! Well, I sent them an email and I think I just put that

I was getting married on Saturday the seventeenth of October and would they like to come. I'm pretty sure I didn't mention Sandra'

'What a plonker you are. So don't blame me. That's typical of a man.' Sarah made to go back in the other room.

'Oi!' James grabbed her arm and dragged her over to a chair.

'What is wrong with you?'

He shoved her down into the chair and stood in front of her menacingly. 'You are going to listen to a few home truths, because I'm fed up with seeing you walking around like a zombie. I know full well that you love Salvatore and he loves you. Any fool could see that in Rome. Now he thinks you're marrying me. You've got to do something about it before it's too late.'

'Too late for what, James?'

'Too late to marry him.'

'I don't want to marry him.'

'I don't believe you, Sarah.'

'I don't care. And you don't bloody care what Salvatore is, do you?' She stood up and shouted at the top of her voice, 'He's part of the Sicilian Mafia. The whole Vasari family is in the Mafia and if you think I'm marrying a Mafia gangster you're sadly mistaken.'

James clapped a hand over her mouth. 'You little idiot, for God's sake shut up.'

'Why? Frightened everyone will hear me?'

'Yes, but not for the reasons you think. None of the present Vasari family has anything to do with the Mafia, either Sicilian or Italian. Carlo told me they had dropped out of anything like that over twenty years ago after his father was shot.'

'But what about the fact that they are fabulously rich?'

'Oh come off it, Sarah. There are plenty of people who are fabulously rich and they aren't in the Mafia.'

But Sarah wasn't satisfied with that answer. 'Oh yeah! And how many of them can afford a private jet? What about all that gear in the hold? What about that so-called business they did in New York and the fact that we were kidnapped? That had to have been a Mafia plot.'

'The gear as you put it is stuff that Carlo needs when he goes out to Africa on behalf of a well-known charity. He's been sinking wells and building houses, schools and hospitals. And he also raises vast amounts of money for quite a number of other charities. And he does it all without public knowledge. All his family are involved and some of his old friends. He said it's payback time for the way they have behaved over the last few hundred years. He told me he'll never let them off the hook and what Carlo says is law within the family and outside it as well.'

He paused to take a breath. Then he carried on before she could interrupt, 'And yes, you are right about a Mafia plot to kidnap Carlo, but they did it to try and get him back into the fold so to speak, but Carlo wouldn't co-operate. It's all been settled now. There won't be any more attempts, but to be on the safe side Carlo is selling his palace in Rome and the villa in Sicily. Soon they will be living somewhere entirely secure and nobody will know where they are. Carlo's family are severing their ties with Italy and going to live somewhere else. Somewhere no one will ever find them. Am I getting through to you?' He grabbed her and shook her.

Sarah started crying.

'You said you would never see Salvatore again, well, you're just about to get your wish, Sarah, because if you tell me one more time you don't love him I will never tell you where they've gone. And that could even be Australia. Who knows?

Maybe Carlo won't even tell me where they're going. This will be your last chance.'

Sarah flopped back into the chair. She couldn't breathe. It felt like a shire-horse had kicked her in the chest. She thought her lungs had collapsed and she gasped for air. It felt like she was having a heart attack and she clutched at her windpipe.

James knelt down in front of her. 'Calm down. You're just having a panic attack. Breathe slowly. Come on. In. Out. In. Out. That's better.'

She clutched his arms. 'When did you get to know all this?'

'I found out a lot while we were being transported to Washington after we rescued Carlo. I admit I was beginning to have my own suspicions and Carlo could see that. He was quite happy to talk about it.'

'Help me. Tell me what to do.'

'If I were you, I'd grab those bags of yours, rush back to Manchester, get your passport and get the next flight to Sicily. You might just catch them. You know I can't go running off to Sicily again. I've got a honeymoon to go on. But don't go alone; take Mark and Pam as company. I'll organize the flight and I'll pay. At least I've found out the reason why you dumped the man who saved your life.'

CHAPTER TWENTY-ONE

'What are you thinking about?' Sarah hadn't spoken for at least half an hour and Mark could see she had something on her mind.

'I was just thinking about the last time we travelled together like this, except we didn't have Pam with us.' She glanced across Mark. Pam was still fast asleep. 'I wish I could sleep like that.'

'Makes you sick, doesn't it? Anyway, what about the last time we travelled together?'

'Remember standing in that cemetery with all those thousands of graves? Most of them were young men, who had given their lives for freedom.'

'And women,' Mark reminded her. 'And then Salvatore nearly died trying to save you. And he did save you. He must have loved you more than life itself. How often do you get someone to love you like that?'

'It looks like we're about to land. Do you want to wake Pam?'

'Yes.' He shook her arm gently. 'Wake up, love. We're about to land. We've got to fasten our seat belts.'

As the plane thundered down the runway, Sarah watched

the familiar mountains of Sicily loom up. They looked almost too close for comfort.

The woman at the car hire counter was an English courier who conveyed some alarming instructions. 'Please take care, Mrs Livingstone. Lock all your doors. Don't stop to give anyone a lift no matter how innocent they look. Don't even stop if you see an accident. Just use your mobile to phone this office. The phone number's at the top of your invoice. We'll inform the emergency services. You'll find the air-conditioning is quite adequate so keep all your windows closed. Don't leave any of your possessions in view and remember to keep the boot locked at all times, even when you're driving.'

It was three o'clock in the afternoon when Sarah drove away from the airport.

'Are you sure you know the way?' Pam sounded anxious. It was obvious the car hire courier had spooked her.

'I'm positive I know the way. Salvatore took me out often enough. Don't worry, Pam. Sicily isn't as dangerous as that courier made out.'

They arrived at Villa Vallerina at half past four.

'Oh no!' Sarah gasped. 'We're too late.'

'How d'you know?' asked Pam.

'Because the gates are wide open and there are no guards.' Sarah drove up to the front of the villa and parked.

'What are we stopping for?' Pam squeaked.

'Jesus, Pam, don't be such a wimp. There's no one around. We didn't even pass anyone on this road.' Mark tried to calm his wife.

'You're not getting out, surely?' Pam was still really nervous.

'Listen, I just want to have one last look round.'

'OK,' said Mark, getting out. 'You stay in the car, Pam.'

But Pam jumped out. 'I'm not staying on my own.'

'Right,' said Sarah. 'I'm going round the back. Mark, you might as well stay by the car. Turn it round, if you like, ready for a quick get-away.'

'For God's sake, Sarah, don't wind her up.'

Quickly Sarah walked round the back. She wanted to visit the place where she had finally told Salvatore all her secrets. The swimming pool had been drained. It looked ghastly. The palms were wilting in their pots and a few scraps of litter fluttered in the breeze. She lingered at the top of the steps leading down to the hidden garden. Time to go home, she said to herself and turned away. But the golden threads of remembrance pulled her back. She wound her way down the steps and through the undergrowth. The immaculate gardens had become a jungle.

A horrid thought crossed her mind. How easy it would be to end her life here in the place where she knew she still belonged to Salvatore. Then she remembered Mark and Pam and what it would do to them. 'I should have come on my own,' she muttered.

She turned the very last corner, stepped down the last step and her heart stopped beating. He was here. The man she loved. Salvatore was here. But something was wrong. The clouds hung motionless. The slight breeze faded away. The world stopped turning. It couldn't be him, could it? It must be a mirage. His head was down on the wrought-iron table. His arm was stretched out across it and he was clutching a moss green silk blouse and that's when she knew it was real and the world started turning again.

'I knew I'd left that blouse behind.' Sarah murmured, smiling to herself.

*

'Oh my God.' Pam grabbed Mark's arm. 'There's a car parked over there behind those bushes. 'Quick, turn the car round and then go and get Sarah.'

'Don't panic, it's probably the estate agent or a gardener.' But Mark could see his wife was terrified so to calm her down they both got back in the car. He'd only just turned it round when another car came flying in through the gates. The gravel flew up as it slid to a halt, bumper to bumper with the hire car.

Pam screamed.

Mark threw himself out of his car at the same time that Carlo and Marilyn Vasari jumped out of their car. After they'd all finished hugging and kissing one another, Mark introduced his wife. He noticed Carlo's flashy Italian sports car was covered in dust. It looked like no one had cleaned it for a year.

Sarah remembered their last time together. She'd been wearing her favourite green blouse with cream slacks. She was wearing those slacks today and a soft cord shirt in that same shade of green. Then she noticed what Salvatore was wearing. Cream chinos and a green shirt! A mirror image of her own clothes. She smiled happily.

'What are you doing here?' Mark asked Carlo and Marilyn.

'Looking for Salvatore. He keeps disappearing.' Marilyn was clearly upset. 'We're very worried about him. We've driven all the way down from Rome. We've been to visit all our old family haunts as well as the places where other members of Carlo's family have homes. No one has seen him. Then we thought he might be here so we took the ferry. We are very frightened. Is he here? Have you seen him?'

'No, but there's a car behind those bushes.'

They all hurried over.

'It's a hire car,' said Carlo, 'but that's his jacket on the seat. He must be here.'

'Sarah's here as well.'

'You're joking,' said Marilyn. 'Sarah and James are here? How could they be so cruel? It will kill Salvatore to see them together.' She looked extremely annoyed.

'They aren't together.'

'What?'

'You lot got hold of the wrong idea. James has married Sandra not Sarah. He realized that he wasn't really in love with Sarah. Good job as well because Sarah was already deeply in love with Salvatore.'

Salvatore suddenly looked up and then he jumped to his feet, but instead of running towards her, he started backing away, towards the wall. The low wall. What was he doing? He looked like he'd seen a ghost.

'Salvatore,' she whispered. Then she shouted, 'Salvatore. No!' But he continued to move back. His legs were up against the wall and for a moment he teetered against it. Then. . . .

'No! No! No!' Sarah screamed, as he fell backwards, over the wall and down to a certain death.

Marilyn still looked slightly confused. 'We knew it was the wedding this week and we've been keeping an eye on Salvatore but he gave us the slip yesterday. We finally realized he might have come here.'

Suddenly the most dreadful screams filled the air. For a few seconds they stared, horrified, at one another. Mark was first off the blocks and the others had absolutely no chance of keeping up with the cricketer as he hurled himself towards the back of the villa. He pounded down the garden and was at the iron gate before the others had even appeared round the corner of the villa. He flew through the gate and down the steps two at a time. 'No, Sarah,' he yelled as he ran towards her. There was no way he was going to let her kill herself, especially not now. He grabbed her round the waist and hauled her off the wall. He pinned her to the ground. 'Don't do it. Salvatore is still alive. He's somewhere in the garden.'

'No, he isn't,' she screamed at him. 'He's just fallen over the wall. Get off me. Let me go.' Sarah was going mad.

Carlo arrived next. He sensed immediately what had happened and he was frantic with terror. He jumped up on the wall and looked for Salvatore.

Then the two women arrived. Their eyes were wide with horror. Meanwhile Sarah was still struggling with Mark.

He just wouldn't let go. She knew she would have to do it. She hit him in the face with her fist, as hard as she could. His nose started bleeding and he had to let go of her. She jumped to her feet and started stripping. Within seconds she was down to her bra and panties. She moved to the wall.

'No!' Marilyn screamed. 'You can't. You mustn't. You'll be killed.'

Sarah knew that in Acapulco they dived from heights of at least 150 feet. This looked like it was a dive of about 100 feet and she thought she could manage it. She was determined to dive in and save him so she climbed up on to the wall.

Everybody screamed and Carlo tried to grab her.

Then Pam suddenly remembered something her mother had told her. 'Stop.' she yelled. 'Leave her alone. She can do it. She's Sarah Simpson.'

'What?' Mark looked up from the ground where he was still trying to recover from Sarah's right-hand jab. 'You mean the diver? Our Olympic gold medallist?'

Sarah had already raised both arms in the air and before

anyone could stop her she had gone. Her fingers were extended and tightly interlocked using what was now considered to be an old-fashioned technique. Sarah wanted to make a safe entry into the sea below. Her arms were protecting her head. It seemed such a long way down. As her fingers touched the water, she steeled herself not to flinch because it was as cold as ice. She felt anxious as she carved a passage through the blackness. It was possible that it wasn't as deep as the locals liked to think and she didn't want to hit her head on any rocks that might be down there. She couldn't see the bottom. She did a somersault and tried to swim back to the surface. Then she started to hallucinate.

She seemed to be suspended in a dark-green glass. There was a crowd on the outside, staring at her. She was really scared and she closed her eyes, momentarily. When she opened them again, the pale faces had gone and she realized it was just a trick of the light. What light? She should be breaking the surface by now but she wasn't. She wasn't scared any more. Maybe I'm dead, she thought. Suddenly she felt warm and calm and happier than she'd felt in a year. She looked for Savaltore but she couldn't see him anywhere and that did make her afraid. Her life was with him and their fate was intertwined. To die without him in her arms was unthinkable.

Something was wrong. There seemed to be hands round her waist and she felt she was being propelled upwards. Her head broke the surface and she was thrown like a piece of flotsam up into the air. She hadn't got time to work out what had happened because in the few seconds that her head was above the waves, she saw him. He was lying face down a few yards away and the current was carrying him out to sea.

'Look!' Marilyn screamed. 'He's there. He's floating out to sea. Oh God. Do something. Someone do something.'

Carlo was already speaking into his mobile.

'Where the hell is Sarah?' Mark was leaning over the wall and Pam was hanging on to his legs for dear life. 'Oh my God. She's there. She's made it.'

Carlo leaned over the wall. 'She won't spot him. He's too far away. It looks like he's dead.'

'Phone the lifeboat service.' Mark grabbed his arm.

'We don't have one.'

'Oh my God. You don't have a lifeboat?'

But Carlo wasn't taking any notice. He was watching Sarah. 'Look,' he whispered. 'She must have seen him. She's going after him.'

Sarah struck out with a powerful freestyle stroke, but she knew that what she was attempting was hopeless. She was a very strong swimmer. It was all down to the accident she had witnessed when she was thirteen. Her parents had taken her on holiday to Blackpool. They were on the seafront and the tide was almost in.

'What the hell are they doing. Oi, you lot. Get back up here,' her father had shouted.

Some boys had apparently slipped under the safety chains so they could go down the steps, leading to the sands. The chains were there for a purpose. They were to stop people going down the steps when the tide was in, but the boys had no idea about that. They were just having a bit of fun, dodging the breaking waves. Suddenly a wave about five feet high swept the three boys into the sea. Her father pushed Sarah and her mother back. 'Get our Sarah away,' he yelled, over the sound of the crashing breakers. Then he ran off to try and get the boys out of the water.

There were about twenty holidaymakers all trying to form a chain. Then the fire brigade and police arrived. Someone must have alerted the lifeboat but it couldn't get near.

Nobody could do anything. The boys had gone.

They read about it in the *Evening Gazette*, that night, in the hotel lounge. The boys had drowned and the bodies had been recovered. That was it. Sarah always remembered how it had cast a terrible cloud over their holiday. They went home the next day, cutting their holiday short by a week. They never went back to Blackpool again, but Sarah never forgot what she'd seen and from that day on she decided to have swimming lessons. First she learnt how to swim properly and then she learnt how to save lives. Then her swimming teacher saw that she had a real talent for diving. And in the end she became the famous British Olympic Gold Medallist, Sarah Simpson.

She'd never had to put her lifesaving skill to the test until today. But it looked like it was too late. She was never going to reach him. The tide was taking him away from her and she couldn't swim as fast as the tide. It was impossible. Everything she'd ever learned about lifesaving had been wasted. She just didn't understand. Surely her talent was meant for just this moment and yet she had failed. Then she heard the voices. They were so hypnotic. They were whispering to her but they were speaking in Italian. Then she heard her mother's voice. 'Go on. Swim to him. You can do it.' Sarah went into the forward crawl. Her arms propelled her through the water. She was kicking her feet only slightly, just enough to stabilize her body. It was a streamlined technique and she felt an incredible strength inside herself, as she raced against the tide.

Back at the villa everyone was leaning over the wall, watching.

'Oh my God!' Mark gasped. Even though he now suspected that Sarah, as well as being a fantastic diver, was also a powerful swimmer, he was still amazed at how fast she was swimming. He blinked his eyes trying to see through the shaft of light that surrounded her. Wait a minute. What was that light? The sun was already setting behind the villa. So where was that bright golden light coming from? More crazy thoughts filtered through his brain. If that was a shaft of sunlight, how come the water all round her was black?

'What's that?' asked Marilyn.

No one answered her.

Finally Mark spoke. 'It's just a trick of the light,' he said. He stood up because the bodies were further out to sea now and he didn't need to lean over the wall to see them. Sarah was closer to Salvatore now but both of them were fast disappearing into the distance. Mark knew that even if Sarah reached him she wouldn't have enough strength to get him back to the beach at Cefalu. He felt sick with grief. He knew he would never see them again and he loved them both dearly. After everything they'd gone through, it just didn't seem fair. His face was wet with tears. They were two wonderful people but now they would never get the chance to make a life together. Yet they would be together in death. They were two lovers walking towards eternity.

'Oh!' Marilyn breathed. 'Look at that.'

Sarah had reached him. She turned him over in the water but he wasn't breathing. She hoisted herself across his body. Then she took a deep breath and placed her mouth directly over his, she blew into it. Another breath. Blow. Another breath. Blow. Another breath. Blow. There was no response. Her feet felt so cold and she flapped them around to try and warm them. She was freezing and then she noticed that the sun had slipped away and it was almost dark. No wonder the water was so cold. She would die in this freezing water. Well, wasn't that what she wanted? To die with Salvatore in her arms?

'No!' she shouted up into the sky. 'Salvatore, come back to me.' She leaned across him and tried again. Blow. Another breath. Blow. Another breath. Blow. Nothing. She looked up and cried out. 'Help me. Mum. Where are you? I'm alone out here and I'm going to die. If there was ever a time I needed you it's now. Help me,' she sobbed. But it was no use. She was numb with cold and exhausted beyond anything she had ever known. 'If you won't help me then let me die with him,' she pleaded. Her prayer was carried away on the wind.

Suddenly she felt an unbelievable warmth spreading up from the black depths and she knew her mother was with her. There was a light all around her. She knew this was the moment. She would kiss him one last time and was reaching for his mouth when she heard her mother's voice.

'My darling girl, try. Try one last time.'

There was a light touch around her waist. Someone seemed to lift her out of the water and it was easy to place her mouth on his. She blew and he spluttered into life.

At the top of the cliff, everyone was watching the beautiful sight of the fishing boats of Cefalu as they sailed out of the harbour. The large lanterns on the bows left an amber trail behind them. They were heading straight towards Salvatore and Sarah. A mysterious golden light encicled them. The oarsmen were rowing as fast as they could and the boats sped along as though they were bewitched.

'How did they know we needed them?' asked Pam.

'I phoned a friend of mine down there,' replied Carlo. 'He owns a hotel. I knew he would get the boats out but I didn't have much hope they'd find them.'

'And they wouldn't have found them if it wasn't for that light,' said Marilyn.

'No, they wouldn't,' agreed Carlo. There was a strange look on his face. 'It may be too late anyway. Come on, let's get down there.' He picked up Sarah's clothes. They ran to the cars and piled in. Carlo set off at break-neck speed. Mark could hardly keep up with him.

'Have you got a licence to drive in Italy?' asked Pam.

'No, but I don't reckon anyone will be looking for drivers without a licence in this particular part of the island right at this moment, do you?'

There were several young men in the boats who stripped off and dived into the water to support the lovers. Within minutes they were both in a boat and being wrapped in blankets. Their rescuers were gabbling away in Sicilian and calling down to the men left in the water. Sarah could only imagine they were complaining about the cold. So why was she so warm? It must have been all the exercise, she thought. She sat in the boat, trying to get her breath back, gazing into Salvatore's eyes. He was alive.

'Where is James?' he asked.

'On his honeymoon with Sandra,' she replied, watching his eyes light up. It was impossible for her to get to him because there were several rowers in between them but she knew there was plenty of time. There was so much time to tell him that she loved him and that she wanted to marry him. She actually felt like she wanted this boat ride to go on forever so she could contemplate the joy that would be hers when his arms enfolded her. She didn't take her eyes off him once and he gazed back at her. She knew exactly what would happen as soon as they were alone. His eyes were telling her.

By the time the boats reached the harbour, Carlo, Marilyn, Mark and Pam were arriving.

'For goodness sake this isn't the Grand Prix,' muttered Marilyn, as her husband skidded to a halt and parked in a cloud of dust. But he hadn't heard her. He leapt out of the car and ran down to the water's edge just in time to embrace his brother and Sarah as they were helped out of the boat.

The whole town followed them to the nearest hotel where as many of them as could get in, crowded round the two survivors. Marilyn pushed forward with Sarah's clothes and she dressed. There was a lot of excited chatter and gesticulations and then Carlo turned to Sarah and said, 'They are all talking about the light.'

'What light?' Salvatore asked.

Sarah kept her thoughts to herself and didn't answer.

'The light that was surrounding you and Sarah,' replied Carlo. He had the same peculiar expression on his face that Marilyn had noticed in the garden at the villa.

The same look was now spreading over Salvatore's face as he listened more intently to all the chatter.

Some of the fishermen came across to Sarah and kissed her passionately first on both cheeks and then on the mouth. The whiff of garlic was quite overpowering, but she didn't care. They must be thanking her for saving Salvatore. She had the impression that everyone knew him.

Pam sidled up to her. 'Well! Well! Well! Aunty Sarah. No wonder you couldn't keep your mind on your work.'

'Rubbish!' Sarah protested. 'I did some of my best designs last year.'

'Maybe so, but they were all in the same colours and you were always muttering something about a Sicilian sunset. Mind you, I do envy you. That man is one hot hunk.'

'Pam! How can you say that when you've got Mark?'

Pam grinned and walked over to her husband. She put an arm around his waist and kissed his cheek. 'Lucky old Aunty Sarah,' she giggled.

'She's nearly as lucky as you,' Mark smirked at her. 'Seriously though, I really thought we had lost both of them.'

Sarah was watching Salvatore. He was holding out his

hand to Carlo. There was a small argument and then Carlo took something out of his pocket and dropped it in Salvatore's hand who put whatever it was in his pocket. Then he came over, took hold of Sarah's hand and, despite protestations from Marilyn, Mark and Pam, dragged her up and pulled her out of the door to Carlo's car. Then he reached into his pocket and brought out two sets of keys. 'The keys to my heart, *cara mia*. This is the key to the villa and this is the key that will take us there. I have always wanted to drive Carlo's sports car.' He grinned. 'He tried to argue, but I told him since I have just come back from the dead he should treat me better.' Then he held up his other hand and there, like a wet dishcloth, was her green silk blouse. He hadn't let go of it not even when he fell from the cliff. He handed it to her then he opened the car door for her.

Sarah got in and her heart was pounding with anticipation. She wondered how long it would take them to get to the villa. And what then?

CHAPTER TWENTY-TWO

Salvatore drove like the devil was after him. He screeched round the bends and whenever he reached a straight piece of road Sarah thought the car was going to take off, but she wasn't in the least bit scared. Everyone on this side of the island was down in Cefalu celebrating. No one would be on the road and anyway she felt impervious to danger. Nothing could touch her now. The hood of the car was down. She held the blouse above her like a flag and whooped with happiness as the wind tried to wrestle it from her.

The car swerved up to the front door. Salvatore leapt out, ran up the steps and unlocked the villa. Sarah followed slowly, savouring every moment. They walked into the hall and he closed and locked the door. Then he took her hand and led her to a bedroom. Sarah knew it had once been his because there was a faint aroma of the sharp, ocean-fresh cologne that he always wore. At the moment all she could smell on his skin was seawater. Quickly she turned to him. She had to ask; it was very important. 'Salvatore, what is that cologne that you always wear?'

He looked at her in amazement. 'What a question to ask me just as we are about to make love. But I will tell you. It is Silver Shadow by—'

'Davidoff,' she finished his answer for him. 'I knew it. I bought some. It was to remind me of you.' She was divinely happy. She knew it was a sign.

'You bought my cologne? What a beautiful thing to do.' He pulled her further into the room.

'Wait.' she gasped. 'Why use Davidoff? Why don't you use Italian cologne?'

'Quite simply because my darling Marilyn, who knows nothing about men's cologne, bought it for me when we first met. And because we all love her, I carried on buying it, just so she would know I liked it. I think it is Swiss. So now you love it and you can buy some for me and I will let you use it. And that will be perfect. And so I answer your questions and now it is time for you to answer my question. Yet it seems you are still trying to delay what will be the most wonderful moment of your life.'

The bedroom was almost empty except for some fitted wardrobes and a bed. Sarah blushed as she realized that there weren't any covers. The bed linen had all been packed, presumably for the move.

Salvatore was howling with laughter. He could read her thoughts so easily. But he hadn't any such hang-ups. 'I have no idea why you are getting so hot because you know I am about to see your gorgeous naked body, Sarah. I've seen it before.'

Sarah blushed even redder. 'You told me you hadn't seen anything.'

'I lied. You were gorgeous. I fell in love with you right at that moment. So I am never going to forget that you dropped that towel and I promise, you are never going to forget tonight.'

Sarah felt her skin was on fire.

He stared deep into her eyes. 'I never did forget you, after we escaped from Cuba, *cara mia* but before we make love I must ask you why you have come back.'

'Because I couldn't forget you, my darling,' she whispered. 'Not a day went by that you weren't in my thoughts. I have been so unhappy.'

'Then why did you let me think you were going to marry James?'

She hesitated because the reason was so terrible.

'The truth, this time, Sarah. I promise it will not change anything.'

'I thought you were in the Mafia,' she whispered miserably.

'Ah! *Sì*! A common mistake on this island especially with a name like Salvatore. Well, Sarah, we almost didn't make it this time. It seems the gods are looking out for us after all. We mustn't squander the time they have given to us today.' He pulled her on to the bed.

'No, we shouldn't squander the time,' she agreed weakly.

Slowly and with infinite tenderness he undressed her, kissing every part of her skin and murmuring words of love sometimes in English but mostly in his own language.

Her fingers trembled with desire as she helped him remove his clothes. She whispered in his ear, 'I love you, Salvatore, more than anything in the world. I want you. I belong to you.'

He drew back. 'No, I understand what you say but I have no wish to own you. You do not belong to me. We belong to each other. We are one. And I will be the one man who never, ever leaves you, my darling Sarah.'

And as he took her in his arms, the fear of seeing him fall to his certain death welled up into a raging burning passion. She took his lips and drank in the sweetness of his tender kiss. She gripped his hips and pulled him close. She caressed his face. She urged him on, moving her body beneath his, tantalizing him, letting him know that she was ready. Her eyes flirted with his and then she lifted her own hips to fuse with his. She gasped at the rush of emotion, when their bodies joined. And when their souls finally bonded, there was an explosion of fire that even Etna couldn't match.

The volcano subsided but she was still in his arms. Her breasts felt soft against his hard chest. Her hips fitted so perfectly into the hollows of his body and he could feel the length of her silky smooth legs; every inch touching his. They were made for each other but how many times had they courted death? He shivered. He had to ask her. Gently he rolled her on to her back and looked into her eyes.

'What did you see out there?'

Sarah knew she wanted no secrets from him even if it was only superstitious nonsense. But it was all a bit of a jumble so she decided to keep it simple. 'I thought I saw some faces but then they disappeared. I thought I felt someone lift me up. Then I saw a light and I felt warm. I think a lot of it was in my imagination.'

He shook his head. 'Why would you think that?'

'Because I heard my mother call to me and she died some years ago.'

'What did she say?' he asked her, softly.

'She told me to try again. Try and revive you. You weren't breathing, Salvatore.' Her voice was full of the anguish she still felt. 'You were dead and I wanted to die with you. It was awful.' Then she burst into tears.

Salvatore crossed himself. 'There is a legend that the servants of the gods live in the caves beneath this villa. They saved you. Everybody talk about it. The fishermen say you are miracle lady.'

Sarah didn't go for this at all but she didn't want to hurt his feelings. 'I don't know about that. I was in such a state I was crying and calling for my mother. I feel she is always with me, watching over me.'

Salvatore nodded. This was something he could relate to. 'Maybe you are right, but tomorrow I take you to see something that will blow your mind away but until then we will make—'

A drumming on the window drowned out the rest of his words. Luckily the bed couldn't be seen through the window. 'Come on. Let us in, Salvatore. You've had quite enough time alone with Sarah.'

Sarah turned beetroot red.

Salvatore just laughed and grabbed his pants. 'Better get dressed, Sarah, but never forget this. Our time together is just beginning.' He planted a kiss on her forehead and departed.

'Salvatore!' Sarah yelled after him. 'You've left your shirt behind.' But he had gone. No doubt he was hoping that his bare chest would give the game away. Strangely enough she found she didn't mind because she wanted the world to know that they were together at last.

Carlo had brought sheets and pillows, obviously borrowed from his friend. 'You might need these tonight when it gets colder. We certainly will.' He enjoyed Sarah's blushes. 'Welcome to the family.' He gave her a passionate kiss on her mouth.

Sarah saw Marilyn raising her eyebrows knowingly and mouthing the words, 'See what I mean?' behind Carlo's back. She was absolutely joyful. 'I couldn't have wished for anything better. Finally a sister-in-law who understands me.'

'You mean a sister-in-law who will help you spend all my money in those dress shops in Palermo and Rome,' laughed Carlo. He'd also brought wine and food and they spent the evening talking about everything that had happened.

'We must tell you, Sarah,' Marilyn smiled. 'Salvatore scoured the shops for green shirts and cream chinos. And none of us can fail to notice you two are dressed in identical clothes today. So what's the story?'

Sarah blushed. I seem to spend all my time red in the face, she thought.

Salvatore spoke up for her. 'These are the colours she wore on her last night in Cefalu. The night James arrived. I wanted so much to remember them.'

'And we thought you'd lost your mind.'

'And I had, Marilyn. I had lost my mind and my heart to an English rose.'

At last the evening came to an end and Salvatore stood up. He took Sarah's hand.

She knew how they were going to spend the night and she couldn't wait to feel his arms around her again, but she was thwarted.

Carlo also stood up. He beckoned to Salvatore. 'Please excuse us, Sarah. I need a word with my brother.'

Salvatore followed him out of the room.

When the two men came back, Sarah looked enquiringly at Salvatore but he just shook his head at her. No matter how hard she tried to quiz him he wouldn't tell her what had been said.

'It's just a little surprise for tomorrow, my darling.'

Then he led her back to his room where they fell into one another's arms again.

CHAPTER TWENTY-THREE

She gazed up at the fresco on the walls of the shrine in the hills above Cefalu and felt her heartbeat quicken because the faces in the painting looked uncannily familiar to her. Maybe she'd seen this painting before. But how could she have? She listened to the old man. He was struggling a bit trying to tell the story in her language but Salvatore had insisted she hear it from someone other than himself.

'This painted by man in 1809. See date here.' The man pointed. 'Is two hundred year ago. He jump to save his *bambina*.'

'His little girl,' Salvatore translated.

'She fall from that place. He say, he see *signorina*.'

'Young unmarried lady,' Salvatore explained. 'You are a *signora*.'

Sarah giggled. 'Yeah! That's right. Old married lady.'

The man continued. '*Signorina* hand child to him. He build shrine as. . . .' He stopped speaking and looked at Salvatore for assistance.

But it was Sarah who answered. 'Thanksgiving?'

'*Sí*. To give the thanks. What is matter, *signora*?' He'd seen the tears in her eyes. 'You see lady? *Sí*?'

'Maybe. I don't know,' she whispered.

'If you see *signorina*, it mean it happen again.' He gave up trying to speak in English and jabbered away in his own language.

Salvatore translated. 'The legend says there are the ghosts of many girls with broken hearts who have not been allowed to marry men they love. The most important bit is written down here, at the bottom of this painting.' He was leaning close to the fresco and reading the minuscule words at the bottom. 'It say the gods of Etna decided that once in every hundred years, a girl who is pure in spirit will be saved. They promise. It is written.' Salvatore turned to Sarah. 'Our friend here says there was another little girl from the town who fell in. A man saw her fall. He didn't even know her. He was maybe a visiting Englishman?'

Sarah could see even Salvatore was struggling a bit. 'A holidaymaker?'

'*Si*. A tourist or just a traveller maybe. He swim out into bay and keep hold of little girl. He was very strong swimmer. But when people dragged them both out of the water he was very scared. He said he saw women floating near him. Little girl say so too. That was in 1909. Marked here under the picture.' He jabbed a finger on the wall.

Sarah leaned closer. She could just make out the numbers scratched on the stone.

'When you dived in you were risking your life to save me. It was a sacrifice born out of love. You could have died. That is the purest sacrifice anyone could make. The spirits of those who have gone before came to your aid. That's it. That's what he was trying to tell you. It's a good job I spend so much time in America, Sarah.' He grinned at her. 'My English is good? *Si*? I teach you to speak Sicilian soon.' He said something to the old man and gave him some money.

The old Sicilian leaned forward and, with a small pointed

knife, he scratched a new date next to the faded one: 2009.

Salvatore kissed her hand. 'Now, we go and eat.'

Over lunch, Salvatore asked her if she believed the legend now.

'I suppose I have to,' she said. She hesitated. There were lots of questions she wanted to ask. But one question was very important.

He read her mind. 'What do you want to ask me, *cara mia*?'

She hesitated. This was a horrible thing to ask. 'If I hadn't been there, were you going to throw yourself in the sea?'

'Ah! Kill myself? No. Is sin against God.' He crossed himself. 'I not need to kill myself. Without you I was already dead, in here.' He stabbed his chest with his finger. 'I was already contemplating selling my business in Venice. All my' – he struggled to find a word – 'all my talent had gone.'

'What business in Venice?'

'I not ever tell you? And you still think it is Mafia business?'

'No! No!' Sarah protested violently. Then she saw he was teasing her.

'I forget I never tell you what I do. I forget you not know anything about me, but we have many years to find out about each other. But this afternoon I will take you and surprise you.'

She laughed and blushed and wriggled her eyebrows at him.

He shook his head at her. 'Not that, Sarah. Not till tonight.'

They were driving through Palermo. Salvatore had been pointing out some famous landmarks. 'Quattro Canti. That mean, the four corners.' They stopped to wait their turn in the traffic jam. 'This is the heart of old Palermo.'

Sarah looked up at the towering grey façade of the building on her right. She guessed it was about a hundred feet high.

Tall marble pillars supported five storeys. Each building was crescent-shaped. If it hadn't been for the streets between them, the four separate buildings would have made a perfect circle. They reared up into the sky, snatching the sunlight from the intersection.

'When those fountains and sculptures were first put there in 1611, it is said they were the colour of pure white marble, like a pearl, you understand? *Sì*? Is the dirt of centuries that make them look so bad.'

They were black with grime. 'They don't look bad at all,' Sarah replied quickly. She wanted to love this city as much as he did for it was the place where he had been born. 'They are amazing and they are so Sicilian.'

'You English, you see beauty in everything here. So romantic, but today I show you something a little prettier.' He had driven through the intersection and was heading down a side street. It was a maze and Sarah had no idea where they were or even if they were pointing north, south, east or west. It seemed Salvatore knew his way around Palermo better than she knew her way around Manchester.

He parked in a small space in a quiet street, full of what looked like very expensive villas. Another car drew alongside and three men jumped out. 'Don't worry, Sarah. These are friends of mine. If I'd been on my own I wouldn't have needed them. Everybody knows I can look after myself. That is how you English put it, is it not? But I wish to protect you, so....' He shrugged his shoulders. 'They can stay here with the car. Come with me, I show you beautiful old house that once belonged to my family.'

Sarah looked up at the massive oak door.

Salvatore unlocked it. 'I get permission from owner to show you around.'

She followed him into a beautiful interior courtyard where

marble statues, stone seats and a graceful fountain begged her to linger a while. There were the usual exotic palms in great big ceramic planters decorated with the most beautiful patterns in the spectacular colours for which Sicily was so famous. Bright blue, buttercup yellow, cherry red and emerald green.

Salvatore had paused to let her take in the beauty of it all, but suddenly she was aware that he was impatient to show her something else. Something more important than a few planters and a fountain.

'This way please.' He walked into a room that could have accommodated at least 200 people. There were fabulous paintings on every wall.

Sarah thought she recognized the artists and she knew instantly they wouldn't look out of place in the National Gallery in London. But then her eyes were drawn upwards. 'Oh my God!' She gasped. 'I have never seen anything so beautiful.'

There was a massive chandelier in the centre of the room. It was truly exquisite. The chandelier was made up of tiny pale-pink roses. Some were fully open. Some were still buds. The roses and their translucent leaves hung from dainty slender stems. The whole arrangement cascaded down in delicate garlands. She knew it was made from glass but it looked as if it was made out of rose-coloured diamonds. It was at least five feet in diameter and must have cost thousands and thousands of pounds.

Salvatore was watching her. 'You like that, Sarah?'

'I love it. I have never seen anything like it. You could hang it in Buckingham Palace and nothing could compare to it. How on earth did you get it in here and how is it suspended?'

'It is attached to a very large metal girder that had to be specially installed. It was a gift of love for my family. It is just a shame that we had to leave it in the house but I have permission to come and look at it whenever I wish.' Salvatore was smiling now. 'You ask me what I do for a living, Sarah, there is your answer.'

'Wow! You sell these?'

'No. I make them from my own designs. For this special one, the pieces were blown in my factory in the heart of Venice. Is just behind Piazza San Marco. Then I assemble it here. Right in this very room. It take me many months to complete.'

Sarah gazed at the masterpiece created with so much love.

'And now we go back to Cefalu where we have a special duty to perform.'

Sarah blushed. She'd never heard it called that before.

Salvatore laughed and the edges of his eyes crinkled. 'Not that kind of duty. You have what they call a one-road mind, *sì?*'

Sarah burst out laughing. 'It's track, not road. It's a one-track mind and yes, where you're concerned, I do find it difficult not to think about' – she paused – 'it.'

'Why don't you say it properly, Sarah? You can't think of anything else except making love and you want to go and make love right now, *sì?* There are twenty-five bedrooms here with beds that all have sheets. But you wouldn't need them because I won't ever let you cover yourself when I make love to you. I want to gaze at your beautiful body forever.'

Sarah was bright red with the conundrum of knowing she wanted Salvatore to make love to her right now and knowing it wouldn't be right to use a stranger's bed.

He shook his head. 'Regretably we have not the time to do as you wish.'

Salvatore stopped the car at the top of the street, which led to the tiny harbour.

'I want you to do something for me and you will have to trust me. I want you to get out of the car and walk down to where the fishing boats are standing. You remember? The place we go on the day James came to Sicily?'

'Yes, I know where you mean. But why?'

'I will tell you when I see you on the beach.'

Sarah wanted to humour him. They had stopped outside a small souvenir shop. For all she knew, he was planning to buy her something. As she set off, she felt like someone was watching her. A man came out of a bakery and dusted some trays down. He put his hand to his forehead in a mock salute and smiled at her. She smiled back. Passing another shop she saw another man had stopped what he was doing and was staring out of the window. All the way to the beach it was the same thing. By the time she'd walked a couple of hundred yards she'd either been saluted, smiled at, or just simply surveyed by about twenty men. If she hadn't known that Salvatore was somewhere near she would have been very, very scared. She'd been on the beach a few minutes when she saw him parking the car. He came strolling down.

'What was that all about?' She suddenly realized that she felt unsettled and it was Salvatore's fault and, it seemed, he hadn't got her a present, he'd just played a trick on her. Maybe he wanted her to find out it how dangerous it was for a woman to walk through Cefalu on her own.

'Sarah! Sarah! I did ask you to trust me.' He could see what she was thinking. 'Come here and sit on the wall. I wanted you to know how safe you will be here in Cefalu. You saw all those men watching you, didn't you?'

'Yes. But I'm not easily frightened; you don't know me,' she snapped.

'You weren't meant to be frightened. All those men are my friends. They thought you were on your own so they were keeping an eye on you. They were keeping you safe for me. All the men of Cefalu and the women as well, young and old alike, will want to protect you from now on. You are a hero.'

'Heroine,' Sarah murmured, correcting him without even noticing she'd done it.

'Ah! *Sí*! The female of hero is heroine. To the people of Cefalu you are the most important person in the world. All of them wish to protect you.'

Sarah felt cheap and nasty at how she had behaved. She started to apologize.

'Is no matter. I had a feeling you would be mad at me. I love it because then your eyes flash fire at me. You must have some Italian blood,' he teased her.

The man they had met in the shrine was waiting for them on the beach. The sun was hanging low in the sky just above the mountains. A boat was already in the water. Salvatore lifted her easily and placed her in it. 'Must not get your expensive Italian loafers wet.'

She laughed. 'These are Marilyn's, I borrowed them.' She sat down on a wooden plank in the bow. 'I could never afford these. Anyway, where are we going?'

'Wait and see.' He took up an oar and said something to the man. Obviously they were going to share the rowing. It was typical of Salvatore. He was so kind and thoughtful. She noticed a bunch of flowers in front of her under another wooden plank and wondered if the man had bought them for his wife.

As he rowed out into the bay, Salvatore asked Sarah to marry him. 'I ask you this now while I am rowing, because otherwise I cover your body with kisses and you would not be able to refuse me. This way, I give you the chance to think about it and refuse me if you want. I give you most beautiful wedding, Sarah. We can get married here in the cathedral, or at the top of the mountain in the ruined Temple of Diana. You can choose. Perhaps you like for us to be married in St Mark's Basilica in Venice. I can arrange it so very easily.'

Sarah couldn't believe that he was offering her St Mark's Basilica in Venice.

'Ah! I do not mean to be so thoughtless. We can be married in England. All your friends are there. Whatever you want you may have. I even give up my factory and take you to live in England if you want. I give you everything you want. I not care where I live. I not care if you still want to make beautiful jewels with James. All I want is for you to be happy. So, is no matter where we live.'

Sarah could tell he was intoxicated at the thought of marrying her because his English was becoming slightly less English. Her heart was beating so fast as she contemplated marriage to Salvatore. Not so long ago she'd been so lonely.

Salvatore was speaking again. 'Carlo take me to one of the sides last night.'

Sarah giggled. 'No, sweetheart. What you mean is, Carlo took you to one side.'

'Ah *sì*! He take me to one side and tell me he want to give to us Villa Vallerina. Is not sold yet. Will be safe for you because you save me. The people here are loyal to me. That is why I make you walk down to beach on your own. So you feel safe.'

Sarah could see the boatman was pointedly ignoring them. He continued to row.

'Not give answer yet. Wait till we throw flowers.'

'What? What flowers?'

'Those. There. Under that seat. We have to thank ladies of the caves for saving us both.'

They were directly under the gardens of the Villa Vallerina but Sarah couldn't see the villa or the gardens. The boatman stopped rowing and the brightly coloured boat drifted slightly nearer to the caves. Both men shipped their oars. Then the boatman lifted the bunch of flowers from under the plank. He spoke to Salvatore in Sicilian.

Salvatore turned to her and said, 'If flowers sink it mean we are both special. We are blessed by the gods. We live happily ever after in Sicily. He wishes you to throw them.'

This is a bit tricky, thought Sarah. She knew that Salvatore was going to be disappointed. Technically speaking, the flowers would float. So, on reflection, she thought it would be a good thing if *she* threw them. Salvatore would make allowances for her, but he would never forgive himself if he threw them and they floated out to sea.

Salvatore held out his hands for the bouquet.

The boatman shook his head and held them out to Sarah instead. 'Do not be afraid, *signora*.' He stared at her.

His eyes seemed to be telling her something else. Something he didn't want to share with Salvatore. He wanted to tell her alone. She took the flowers from him wondering at their weight. Suddenly she realized what the boatman had done; he's put something else with them she thought, trying not to laugh. Good God! There must be at least a couple of pounds of lead here. She stared at him.

He stared back innocently.

OK, play the game, Sarah. Throw the flowers under the cliff. She stood up and Salvatore moved close to her. He put his arms round her waist so she wouldn't fall. She knew these flowers would sink like a rock. She threw them in the general direction of the caves. But, as they hit the water, a shaft of sunlight from the setting sun surrounded the flowers and they floated for a few moments in a pool of gold. Then they sank rapidly below the inky black water. Wait a minute! How could they have floated? And where was that golden light coming from? She looked up. You couldn't see the sunset from here. It was setting behind the villa. She looked down. The water was black. There was no light on it at all. What was going on?

A woman's voice whispered, 'Sometimes you think you have all the answers, my darling girl, but you don't. Choose well and you will be happy at last, my dear child.'

She knew instantly that her mother was speaking to her. She was telling her she should choose Salvatore. Sarah turned to Salvatore, threw her arms around his neck and burst into tears of happiness. They sat down on the wooden plank.

The boatman took up both oars and started rowing.

'Where are we going?' Sarah could see the twin towers of Cefalu Cathedral receding into the distance. The boatman was taking them out to sea. She wasn't keen on going too far out.

Salvatore kissed the top of her head. 'No problemo! We just go little way so you see the sunset better,' he soothed her. 'You are safe with me. You are not cold, *cara mia*?'

'I won't be cold if you keep your arms around me,' she said, leaning against him.

'What you thinking about, Sarah?'

'Marriage to you, Salvatore.'

'You wish to tell me your answer now?'

'Of course I want to marry you.'

The boatman turned the boat towards the harbour.

Sarah was suddenly breathless with the beauty that was spread out for her approval. Lamplight spilled across the water. Behind the town the mountains were edged with dark orange. The sunset had turned the black waves to molten gold. As they drew nearer to the town she heard someone singing. It was a famous aria from *Tosca*. It was one of her favourites. And she suddenly knew that this was where she wanted to spend the rest of her life. At the Villa Vallerina. She would always be able to watch the sun setting over Cefalu, with the man she loved.

She looked up into his face. He was so beautiful. He would never be able to tame those wild black curls no matter how much hair gel he used. His blue eyes melted her heart as he smiled that warm infectious smile. She smiled back at him. 'I love you more than anyone in the world. I know we will always be happy. Yes, I will marry you as long as you promise me something.'

'I give you anything you ask.'

'I want to get married here in Cefalu and I want to live here in Cefalu. I want to give up my work. There are plenty of people to take over. People who need a job and a chance to make something out of their lives like Lizanne. She is every bit as talented as me. So, that's it, my darling. I want to stay here forever. Here where I can always see the beautiful sunsets of Sicily.'

'You bring me so much joy.' He bent his head and gave her a long lingering kiss. 'We stay here so you will always see the sunset because the gods will paint it for you every night. But you will never see one more beautiful than this. This is the sunset when you have pledged yourself to me: this is our Sicilian Sunset.'